THE BRIGHT SIDE

A FLIPPIN' FANTASTIC ROMANCE

LUCY BEXLEY

SYNOPSIS

Darby lives her life on the bright side. She loves her two best friends Mia and James, so much in fact that she's built an awesome career running Flippin' Fantastic Renovations with them. All she wants is to decorate houses, cheerlead the people around her, and for no one to call her by her given name (Jane).

Astrid West is restless. She's curated a life that ties her to nothing and no one. Her best friend is a stray cat named Meatball. She works a series of part-time jobs and owns exactly 8 shirts, all of them black. She's lived in Denver for a year and has yet to commit to a lease. She moves cities on a whim, always looking for that perfect location where everything will fall into place.

Astrid is working the door at Revel, a Denver lesbian bar, when she meets Darby. Darby, who wears mittens and pink heart sunglasses and offers to help her, a total stranger, move apartments on New Year's Day. Can Darby convince Astrid that people make a place a home? Or will Astrid leave Denver in search of greener grass before she gets the chance?

The Bright Side is the final novella in a trio of Flippin' Fantastic

romances about the three women who own and operate Flippin'
Fantastic Renovations. Put on your heart-shaped sunglasses and
curl up with this lesfic romantic comedy for the perfect cure to your
February blues.

This book is for anyone who's worked to pull themselves out of a dark place. And for all those who helped them along the way.

CHAPTER ONE

IT'S A LOVE STORY

DARBY

"All the best friendships are love stories." Darby's voice had the buoyancy of a hot air balloon.

"But isn't the point of tonight to start real love stories, Darbs?" Mia looked like a runway model, her skin a striking contrast to her cream coat and fluffy hat.

"The point of tonight is for James to talk to some women who aren't us and for you to get back on the horse or mechanical bull or whatever."

Mia widened her eyes. "Ok, that was one time, and it was *your* birthday."

"God, that was a great night! I wonder if I still have the pictures." Darby reached for her phone, but Mia caught her wrist and shook her head in a slight yet threatening manner.

"I talk to Nora all the time," James huffed.

"I think Darby means human women, babe, not your cat."

"And *I* think I deserve a friendship award. I can't believe you talked us into speed dating. And that the theme is 'love at first line'. Mia, we're losing our edge." James raised an eyebrow and pulled her flannel shirt tighter around her thin frame.

"My offer to make you both friendship bracelets is still on the table. I've been working on my beading skills." Darby linked one arm through James' and one through Mia's, resisting the urge to skip. Linking arms always felt distinctly like traversing the Yellow-Brick-Road. James shivered next to her. "Where's your coat, James?"

"It's in my truck. I didn't realize this place was a mile away."

Mia quirked an eyebrow at James. "To be clear, you were too cool to wear a coat, but decided the flannel and insulated work boots were fine for tonight?"

"I just didn't want to deal with a coat all night. It's awkward." James shrugged.

Darby came to a halt in front of the speed dating sign and did her best Vanna White reveal. "Well, lucky for you, we can go inside before you freeze!"

"Wait." James crossed her arms over her chest and took a step backward toward the street. "You didn't mention it was at a club."

Darby threw an arm around James' shoulders and reeled her back in "Revel's not a club, per se."

The door flew open and a woman in all black stepped outside. The booming base ricocheted into the night air.

James cleared her throat.

"Ok, look," Darby said, going into damage control, "if you hate it we can all just hang out together. Have a pal's night. We can celebrate the stunning, perfect, absolutely incredible house Mia found us to flip."

"Have you been practicing your superlatives again, Darby?" Mia arched a perfect dark brow.

"No need to practice. I've perfected them."

James snorted a laugh.

The woman in all black pulled a beanie from the back pocket of her dark jeans and settled onto a wooden stool by the door. She was built like a dockworker. Strong and compact. Every inch of her 5′6 frame looked like she could throw Darby over her shoulder and run for a mile. Maybe later. For now, her goal was getting James inside and with a name tag.

The heat of the bar engulfed them instantly, fogging Darby's glasses. Winter was the one time she was more blind with her glasses than without them, and she was not legally allowed to operate heavy machinery without them. She removed the frames and cleared the lenses with the hem of her sweater, squinting into the mood lighting of the space. It had the faint red and purple glow of a boardwalk fortune teller. James was going to hate it.

She slipped her glasses back on and wrapped a hand around James' wrist before she could disappear to the bar, leading them over to the card table for check-in.

A woman covered almost entirely in red sequins smiled at them from behind her clipboard. She looked like a mermaid and Darby was here for it.

"Hi, my friends and I would like to check in for speed dating!"

"Like is a strong word," James mumbled beside her.

Darby glanced to Mia for backup, but she was frowning at something on her phone. Maybe tonight she'd stage an intervention to get her off social media for good. Too much time spent comparing yourself to others didn't leave enough time to appreciate all the good stuff. Like your best friend who found the most amazing speed dating event.

"Perfect! We'll get started in about twenty minutes, so I'll get you checked in and then you can grab a drink while you wait. We've got a few specials tonight. What's your name?"

"I'm Darby."

The woman scanned her list. "Oh, there you are. Sorry, we organized it by first name." The woman handed her a name tag that said Jane D.

"Oh, could we change this? No one calls me Jane."

Mia looked up from her phone. "It's fine, Darbs. That's only because you think people will confuse you with James. You are the only person worried about this."

Darby grimaced. Getting used to going by her last name had been strange at first. But James' name suited her so well that the only thing that made sense to her was to pick a different name.

The woman held out a sharpie and Darby sighed in relief crossing out the Jane on her nametag and writing in Darby in neat letters. She added a smiley face for good measure.

James and Mia got their names and then they headed to the bar. The event would start at eight and the New Year's Eve festivities would begin at ten. A perfect evening where Darby didn't have to worry about Mia scrolling sadly through her Instagram at home. Instead, she could observe her sadly scrolling her phone next to her at the bar.

"This place looks great, don't you think?" Darby asked, turning to her friends.

"It's got a very Gatsby's final party vibe." James glanced around at the gold decorations.

"Yeah, it's nice."

"Should we come up with a plan for speed dating? Do you two want a signal in case you're both interested in the same woman?"

"I don't think that will be a problem," James said with a slow smile. "What about you? Do you want a signal?"

"Me? No, I'm not really looking to meet anyone tonight."

Darby's friends looked at her with expressions that hovered between blank and murderous. "Then why are we *here*?" Mia asked at last.

Darby took a deep breath. The hard part was over. The hard part being getting her friends through the door of a New Year's Eve speed dating event. "I thought you both could use a bit of excitement!"

"I see you're confusing torture with excitement again, Darbs."

DARBY LIKED to think of herself as someone who could talk to paint drying, and for the past thirty minutes, she'd felt like she'd done just that. Usually, she was the one who exhausted people, but after her most recent conversation with a depressed writer obsessed with old-timey circuses, she was ready to tap out. Maybe James and Mia had been right, speed dating was not "fun".

She glanced around and saw Mia settling down across from a white woman with messy blonde hair who threw her head back and laughed at something Darby felt sure Mia hadn't meant to be funny. Mia cringed behind her smile.

She scanned the rest of the space and saw James at the bar. At least everyone was accounted for. She could take a few minutes to reset and figure out how to still make the best of this night.

THE COOL RUSH of Denver air hit Darby as she pushed outside. She winced as the smell of cold burned in her nose before adjusting to something pleasant, akin to a campfire. She leaned back against the brick wall of the building, rummaging in her bag.

"I'm going to have to ask you to do that 100 feet from the entrance."

Darby startled and looked up to see an apologetic smile softening the features of the bouncer's face. She was standing just outside the light of the door, and in her night watchman garb, Darby had missed her completely. The calm she'd felt at stepping outside wound itself into a low anxious knot like nerves before a performance.

"Oh, um, okay." Was it a fire code thing, not having

people near the entrance? She glanced around but didn't see anyone else on the street. Not surprising, as her breath was all but crystalizing in front of her face. Darby took a few distracted steps away from the door as she continued ransacking her bag. Was it possible James had the right idea with her pockets only shtick?

"Do you need a light? I think there are matches inside, though good luck with this wind."

"Oh, no, I'm not—" Darby interrupted her own train of thought by pulling out her inhaler and triumphantly holding it up in the air for the bouncer to see.

The woman let out a laugh. "You know, I think those are still legal to use indoors."

"True, but hard to recover from, socially speaking." Darby took a deep hit from her inhaler, holding the medicine in.

"Oh right, speed dating's tonight. How's that going? Did you meet anyone interesting?"

"Sure, lots of people were interesting! But I'm not really looking to meet anyone. I kind of dragged my friends here to find dates for New Year's Eve. One is recovering from a breakup and the other... could use some company, I think. Tonight seemed like the perfect time for a dual intervention."

"Are you not looking because you already have a date?"

Why did the conversation keep returning to her? Darby pulled her open jacket more tightly around herself, turning fully to face the woman in black. "No, I just like to be alone. I've got my friends and a lot of hobbies." Darby shrugged. "I'm happy."

"Happy people can date too, I think. Not speaking from experience, obviously." The woman pulled the beanie from her head and ruffled her jet black hair, not quite long enough to tuck behind her ears.

The woman took a few steps closer to Darby, absolutely studying her chest. She was torn between wanting to curl in on herself and basking in the glow of her attention. In the end she took another discrete puff of her inhaler.

"I'm Astrid, by the way."

"I'm Darby."

"Oh, so that's what your nametag says. I couldn't make it out in the dark. I was trying to figure out if you were Jane with a line through it like when Prince was a symbol."

"Yes, I'm the lesbian formerly known as Jane."

"So, your name is Jane? Or you stole Jane's speed dating identity and I'm going to get a call in twenty minutes that they found her unconscious in the coatroom?"

"Does that happen a lot here?" Darby laughed. "Jane is technically my name. But I go by my last name for logistical reasons."

"Say more."

Darby shrugged. "My best friends are Mia and James. James and Jane sound a lot alike. Like *a lot*. It started when we waited tables together and just kind of stuck."

"But what about now? How much time do you spend with James?"

"Well, we're best friends and we own a company together. If James and Mia would let me I'd get us a house where we could grow old together in Golden Girls bliss. Except more like Golden Gays, I guess."

Astrid laughed. "Wow, that's... something. So, your friend claimed the J name, and you had to pick an alternate? Why not them?"

"I volunteered. Jane is just—" Darby shrugged. "Well, you know, plain Jane. Jane of all trades. Et cetera." She waived her hand in a circle. "But James' name is perfect for her. You'll see."

"Why would I see?"

"I suspect they'll send a search party for me before long. I snuck out during the lightning round."

"Oh, well, I don't want to keep you from your friends."

"I thought I was keeping you."

Astrid held Darby's gaze, her dark eyes were kind, but the edges held a sadness like worry lines that had yet to form. "Yes, you are keeping me from my very busy job of guarding this door. I think I have about fifteen more minutes until the pre-midnight New Year's Eve rush hits."

"Okay then, fifteen minutes." Darby put a finger to her chin. "Tell me your New Year's resolution."

"I don't have one."

"Great! Then now is the *perfect* time to make one."

"Tell me yours first."

Darby nodded and moved a few inches closer to Astrid. "First, I want to take a tarot reading class. And I want to work on my pottery. I've already got another cooking class lined up. And I want to volunteer more. Besides just at the food bank and library book sales, I mean. And I want to find my friends love, but I can basically check that off after tonight! Okay, Astrid, it's your turn."

Astrid removed her hat again and ran her palm over the buzzed hairs on the back of her head. "I guess it's to make my new apartment a home. I never really settled into my old place."

"That's a great resolution! I can totally help! I do interior decorating for the company I own with my friends. How long have you been in your new place?"

"Negative one day. I move in tomorrow. I'm not sure why I thought January first was a good day to move in Denver. With my luck, I'll probably be walking my stuff over in a blizzard."

"What do you mean walking your stuff over?"

"My truck rental fell through and I haven't found a reliable way to secure boxes to the back of my motorcycle. It's only like ten blocks from my current place."

"You're not going to walk boxes, silly. I'll help you move. Give me your address."

"Oh, no, you don't have to." Astrid's eyes went wide, and the streetlight highlighted the tears in them.

Probably the relentless wind. How did she do this job and not freeze completely?

Two women were approaching the bar in a haze of raucous laughter with their arms linked. Astrid glanced at them and took a step toward the door.

"I'm serious, you know. Give me your address, I'll help you move." Darby tore her name tag from her shirt and pulled a pen from her bag.

Astrid hesitated before grabbing the pen and scribbling down a street address then handed them back.

Darby stuck the sticker on the back of her phone. "See you tomorrow, Astrid."

"Right, okay. Happy New Year's Jane Darby."

CHAPTER TWO

THE TRUCK BED

ASTRID

ASTRID KICKED A BOX ACROSS THE FLOOR AND SHOVED HER hands into the pockets of her fleece track pants. She shivered in her white t-shirt and squinted at the thermostat. How can sixty-two feel like beach weather after four months of winter, but absolutely arctic when it's inside her apartment? Shouldn't temperatures adhere to some standard rule of physics or whatever? She fiddled with the thermostat until the knob detached in her hand. Perfect. Add that to the towering stack of reasons she was ready to leave this horrible place.

She slipped on her sherpa-lined denim jacket and breathed into her hands to warm them. It was still early, but she might as well get started hauling her few boxes to her new place. At least she owned almost nothing. Her clothes fit neatly into her dad's old army duffle bag. She could do this alone—how hard could it be to carry a few books and records to her new place?

There was no point in waiting for Jane. Or Darby. Or whoever she was. That offer to help her move was pure drunk-woman-in-a-bar-bathroom energy. But still, Astrid couldn't shake the slightly uncomfortable warm feeling the offer put in her chest. Like a loose floorboard that gave way a bit more each time she tread across the memory of their conversation. Feeling cared for, even fleetingly, was kind of nice.

They were an interesting trio, not the carbon copies of each other some friends are. James, the proud owner of the group's only J name for some reason, was tall and kind of butch but with her edges sanded down. Her face when she'd stepped out of the bar to collect Darby, was bewildered but kind. Even if her fair complexion was a little ethereal in the street lights. Darby's other friend, Mia, was it? Was a stunning Black woman, her umber skin complimented by her charcoal black hair. More runway than Revel. And then there was Darby, flushed pink cheeks glowing on her ivory skin, dancing in circles through Astrid's mind. Not that Astrid needed to remember the names and faces of people she'd probably never see again.

She had liked the way the few snowflakes that fell last night caught in Darby's dark curly hair like fairy lights.

A knock on the door startled her. Probably the jerk landlord here to tap on his watch and remind her she needed to be out today.

She squared her shoulders and walked to the door. She debated flicking the chain open so he could get a good look at the boxes and leave her alone, but in the end, she left it in place.

She was not met by a stout Italian man on the other side of the door. Instead, it was like opening it to Narnia. There in the flickering light of the dingy hallway was that mess of curly hair once again glittering with snow.

"Hi, is this an okay time?" Darby pointed to herself, a huge smile on her face. "Darby, from last night."

Darby looked incredible in her dark jeans and cute wool

coat. Was that lipstick? Standing in front of her, Astrid felt like a pile of dirty laundry.

Astrid cleared her throat, willing her shocked expression to fade. "Yeah, I know who you are, I just didn't think you'd come."

"Oh." Darby tilted her head to the side and met Astrid's gaze in the fractionally opened door. "Why not?"

"Hold that thought." But what she really meant was *forget it*. Astrid hastily closed the door with an unsettling bang and removed the chain before opening it again wide enough for Darby to enter. "Come in."

"I got a killer spot right out front. Why didn't you think I'd come to help you move?"

"Well, you were at a bar last night and it's New Year's Day. I thought it was just a fake but well-meaning thing like saying 'let me know if you need anything' or asking someone how they are."

"Are those usually not real things?"

"'How are you?' is like a figure of speech. You say it but what you expect to hear back is good or fine."

"I think I've been doing those conversations wrong."

Astrid couldn't hold back her laugh at the genuine angst on Darby's face. "You're one of a kind, Darby." She made her way to the bare window and peered out. "Is that your pickup truck?"

"It's James', but I borrowed it." Darby wrapped her arms around herself and squinted at the place on the wall where the thermostat once resided.

"Do you two actually live together?"

"I wish. No, we traded last night. You should have seen her driving away in my little car."

"So you were always planning on coming this morning to help me? You had to coordinate for it." There was that creaky floorboard of emotion again. Astrid tried not to flinch from the unexpected pang in her chest. She must be more tired than she thought.

"Yeah, my car doesn't fit much—but that might have been… okay." Darby looked around at the sparse boxes. Astrid had to admit, the place looked like a grocery store before a snowstorm. Empty but for the chaos.

"Aren't you freezing?" Darby pulled a hat from her pocket and pulled it on.

"Sorry about that. The thermostat broke this morning. My new place has heat though. At least I hope it does."

"It just came off the wall? Do you want me to fix it?"

"Nah, this place is the worst. Inhospitable to its core."

"Sure, but I don't want you to get charged for it. Let me go get James' toolbag from the truck, I'll be right back."

"It's really—" But Astrid was talking to herself as she watched Darby skip out of the apartment.

She wandered over to the window and watched as Darby reappeared on the street a few moments later. And yup, still skipping. Should she be afraid? At what point did excessive cheer become threatening?

Darby had the thermostat repaired and the heat clicking on within minutes. "There, that's better. And now you might get your security deposit back!"

Astrid was stunned into silent awe. It was inexplicable that this woman should care about her security deposit or that she was here at all. Not unpleasant, just mystifying. "Has anyone ever mentioned that you are, like, forcefully kind?"

"Of course, all the time!" Darby's face fell. "Oh wait, are you saying that because you hate it?"

"No, I'm just… adjusting."

"Ok, should we move stuff while you adjust, or would you like some time?"

Of course, Darby was here to do her a favor. And Astrid should be falling at her feet in thanks because she had absolutely no plan besides walking over a few boxes at a time using the dolly she'd stumbled upon in the super's office. Quite literally stumbled upon and fell on her face after picking the lock to see if she could find some spare light bulbs to replace the ones having a 90s rave in the hallway. In retrospect, it would have been easier to go to the hardware store. But where's the fun in that?

"You know what? I've suddenly become well adjusted. Any ideas on where we should start?" Astrid looked over, but Darby was already halfway across the apartment peering into her room.

"Let's start with the hardest thing first, that way the rest of the move is smooth sailing! It's like eating your vegetables so you can get to your pizza."

"Who eats pizza with their vegetables?"

"It's a thing people do. Don't worry about it. So, I think let's start with the mattress."

"Let's come back to that, actually. I'm not sure it will fit down the stairs. It might be a casualty of the move."

Darby looked like she was trying to solve a complicated equation. She walked to the door and opened it to lean into the hallway. "But it has to fit. How did it get up here?"

"I hired four guys and there was still a lot of swearing. I think I might just cut it into pieces and put it in trash bags." Astrid paused and tilted her head. "I just heard how that absolutely makes me sound like a 70s serial killer. Which I am *not*, by the way."

"Of course you're not. It's not the 70s. Maybe we could lower it out those windows if you have some rope."

"That has the potential to actually kill someone."

"Good point. Stairs it is!"

"It's not moving. I think we should leave it here. You can save yourself—escape to brunch." Astrid's voice was choppy with exertion. The mattress was good and truly jammed between the steps and ceiling of the curved stairway. She was trapped in moving purgatory with the absolute nicest stranger she'd ever met. Probably there were worse ways to perish.

"We can't leave it, what will you sleep on?" Darby's voice was muffled by the bed separating them, making the few stairs below sound like a far off land.

"An air mattress. Is that a bad idea?"

"My mind says no but my back says yes. Come on, we've almost got it."

"Fine," Astrid grunted, throwing her shoulder into the wall of unmoving concrete that was recently the most comfortable bed she'd ever owned. Darby's surprised yelp echoed off the tile.

"Are you okay?"

"Totally fine, my hand just got caught for a second."

"Great, now I've maimed you. I'm going to see if anyone on my floor has a chainsaw."

"For the sake of everyone's safety, I really hope no one does. Come on. You can do it, put your back into it." Darby sang the last part.

"I know you did not just quote an Ice Cube song to me as motivation."

"I think that song has a positive mindset."

"Fine, on the count of three I'll push as hard as I can while you pull."

"That's the spirit!"

The mattress dislodged and flew like a sled down the rest of the stairs. Astrid looked on in horror both trying and not trying to spot Darby's form flattened on the stairs like a cartoon piano victim. But she had tucked herself against the wall and was smiling brightly in a way that made Astrid feel a few inches taller.

They wrestled the mattress through the building door and across the icy sidewalk. The snow was still falling lightly in the gray morning as they heaved the mattress into the bed of Darby's borrowed truck.

Darby climbed in after it, falling back onto the soft surface arms and legs snow angeled.

"Huh, a bed in a bed. Do you think that's why they call it the bed of the truck?" Darby dug in the pocket of her coat and pulled out her inhaler.

"Maybe." Astrid climbed up next to her and gently laid down beside her. "I'm dying."

Darby's voice overlapped her lament. "It's gorgeous."

For the first time, Astrid looked up at the snow. Large white flakes floated down from the sky like a burst feather pillow. It was, in fact, gorgeous. "You're right, it is. Do you always notice things like that?"

"Things like the weather? Sure, when it falls right on me." Darby held her hand into the air to collect a few snowflakes before studying them. She turned toward Astrid on the bed, her hair messy and splayed out, her breath still settling from the exertion. The street around them was quiet, and it was almost unbearably intimate, laying beside her like that. "So," Darby said brightly, "what are we moving next?"

"Nothing. No more moving. We live here now."

"You know, I've never spent this much time with a woman and a bed and not at least gotten her breakfast after."

"Are you proposing what I think you are?"

"I am." Darby grinned. "Waffles."

CHAPTER THREE

SAY IT'S A 911

DARBY

D**ARBY BOPPED TO THE LAST FEW NOTES OF** *R**UN** A**WAY WITH** M**E*** as she parked James' truck alongside the curb of the house they were currently flipping. She killed the engine and glanced at the pink Post-it note James had laminated to the dashboard with packing tape. The black marker was a little faded from the sun, but she knew it by heart.

Darbs, if you are reading this, please turn the volume on the radio way, way down. Like lower than you think is reasonable. And I am begging you to change the station. I can't start one more day being assaulted by Carly Rae Jepsen. Please and thank you.

Darby had added her own little heart at the bottom of the note, and while James had complained about it, it was still there. She restarted the truck and switched the station to one where a cowboy was singing about loving his truck. Appropriate.

The house was dark. Suspiciously so, as it was eleven a.m. and twenty minutes ago when she'd called to get James' coffee order, she had assured Darby that she was here work-ing. She set the drinks on the porch, her liter of Frappuccino towering over James' small black coffee. Coffee should be at least half sugar, but she didn't have the heart to tell James that.

She did her signature knock to the beat of Call Me Maybe and shivered on the porch as she waited for James to open the door. She scooped up the coffees, grateful for the warmth of James' cup. It might basically be motor oil, but it was keeping her hands warm.

The house was as silent as the day they'd found it, except for fewer mice stirring, hopefully. Darby squinted at her reflection in the window as she tried to detect any sign of life. When had James put up curtains and why were they so ugly? The entire point of Flippin' Fantastic Renovations was trying to increase the house's appeal, not to haunt it. She glanced over at the neighbors just in time to see a pair of binoculars duck behind the fence like someone had whacked the watcher in the head with a mallet. Darby waited for the head to pop back up a few feet away like the moles in the game, but it didn't. By the third time she'd hummed through Call Me Maybe, she accepted that extreme action was needed to get James to open the door. She juggled the coffees to one side and took off her mitten to unlock her phone.

"Hey babe, is something wrong? I'm about to head into a client meeting." Mia sounded a little breathless.

"Nope, totally fine. But can you do me a favor?"

"Sure, what is it?"

"Can you text James and tell her to call me? Say it's a 911."

"Darby, my love, I hate to tell you this, but you're on your phone right now. Why don't you do it?"

"You know the 911 rule—"

"Don't text 911 unless you've also dialed 911 and an ambulance is on the way." Their voices overlapped like a Double-Dutch chant as they parroted James.

"This is why you shouldn't have cried 911 to trick James into showing you her bad haircut, Darbs."

"I would have died if I didn't get a picture of that, and you know it."

Mia's laugh over the phone was like the sun breaking through the clouds. "That picture is incredible. I have mine framed. So, what's the emergency?"

Hearing her friend happy sent warmth through Darby's chest. "I'm at the house and she won't answer the door."

"Thaaaaaat's not an emergency." The click of Mia's heels was a steady percussion in Darby's ear.

"I also drank a lot of coffee and have to pee."

"Okay fine, but the wrath of James is on you."

"You're the best! Call us after your meeting!"

They clicked off and Darby clutched her phone, bopping her head as she waited for it to ring.

"Hey, James Dean!" Darby's words sent bright white puffs of air in front of her face.

"Hi." James sounded out of breath. "Are you okay? Are you hurt?"

Darby squinted as she tried to make out James' words. Maybe they had a bad connection. "Why are you whispering?" She asked loud enough for James to hear through the maple door. "Can you let me in the house?"

From behind the side fence, Darby heard the binoculars person mutter something that sounded like an expletive-laden "I knew it!"

The door to the house opened slowly and James closed her eyes against the bright sun.

"Were you just standing by the door the whole time? Why is it so dark in here?" Darby handed James her coffee and made her way into the dark cave of the living room.

"I was just, um, laying low for a bit," James mumbled.

"Right, but *why*?" Darby booped James' nose as she passed her. She pulled aside the drop cloth that had been nailed over the window. An atrocity. Dust clouded the sunbeam making its way into the room.

"Fine, the neighbor next door has been giving me a hard time about permits and she came over and knocked after some lumber got delivered and I just couldn't deal with her."

"Well, just tell her we have the permits."

"I tried but she keeps citing very specific codes and it's tripping me up."

"Do you want me to talk to her? I'm sure it's a misunderstanding!"

"No, please don't do that."

"Okay, okay, show me what you've been up to besides making the place look like a Spirit Halloween store on November first."

JAMES WALKED Darby through the house. They stepped over rolls of orange shag carpeting that had been peeled back to reveal hardwood floors through most of the house. James' eyes lit up as she talked about the wide planks and gorgeous grain. If only she could channel that confidence and enthusiasm about animate objects as well.

A knock on the front door interrupted their comparison of shades of gray paint just as Darby was about to explain again why all the cool grays like Slightly Charred Campfire Marshmallow are wrong for the space, but a warm gray like Hot Stones or Meditation would work. A split second of relief flashed across James' face before she ducked her head and made an excuse about checking on the boiler.

The woman on the porch was exceedingly pretty. Her puffy coat and bright red hat made Darby want to go ice skating and drink hot chocolate, and then watch Legally Blonde for the one millionth time. Darby remained silent, waiting for the woman to speak until she couldn't take it anymore.

"Hello! I'm Darby. What can I do for you?"

"I know who you are." The woman's voice held an edge like the business end of an icicle.

"Oh." Darby cocked her head to one side, feeling a swell of guilt that she'd met and forgot this woman. "I'm so sorry about that! Some days my memory is just not what it used to be. How do we know each other?"

"I'm Zee. I live next door."

"Oh, Zee, of course! I didn't recognize you without your binoculars!"

"Wow, you're even worse than the tall one that's avoiding me." Zee thrust forward the papers she had been clutching in her hand.

"I didn't mean to upset you. It's just that every time I see you, you're sort of hiding. Did you need James for something?"

"I don't need any of you to do anything besides to stop whatever you're doing. That's a noise petition. You'll see it has the requisite number of signatures."

Darby flipped to the last few documents, scanning signature after signature. "I didn't realize so many people were upset about the noise."

"Well, they are. Be done by five." Zee turned and slingshotted back to her house like an angry bird, the ball on her red hat catching the wind.

"Wow, she sounded pissed," James said, coming up behind her.

"I guess the noise is bothering a lot of people. So maybe she's upset on their behalf."

James took the papers Darby was flipping through and tossed them on the floor. "There's no way one hundred people can even hear the noise of me working, let alone be bothered by it. Let's just ignore it."

"We can't ignore it, it's a legitimate petition, James."

"Some of those signatures might as well have been in crayon. Who uses a purple pen?"

"I do." She turned to James, trying her best to look indignant.

"Oh, right, sorry Darbs. You know what I mean."

"I think we should make it up to her—maybe get her a gift. Do you know what she likes?"

"How would I? Let's just get her a fruit basket or something generic." James twisted the toe of her work boot on top of the papers like a cigarette she was trying to snuff out.

"But we don't even know if she likes fruit. Or if she's allergic to anything. Remember how last year I started having issues with pineapple and now my mouth goes numb whenever I order a bananarama smoothie?"

"Ok, fine. I'm sorry that happened to you, I know how much you miss those smoothies." James placed a comforting hand on Darby's shoulder. "But she doesn't even have to eat the fruit. The fruit is just a gesture. Isn't it the thought that counts?"

"Yeah, but that's only true when you actually put some thought into it."

"Oh damn, I didn't know that. Maybe we should get her a case for her binoculars, so she can put them away sometimes."

"That's actually not a bad idea. We could get it monogrammed!"

CHAPTER FOUR

CALL ME MAYBE

ASTRID

It was usually around eleven p.m. that Astrid started reconsidering every decision she'd ever made. Like why in the hell she was working three jobs, two of which had her outside in the winter. The cold had seeped into her bones. She felt stiff, like her bones were made of glow sticks just waiting to be cracked. She liked her daisy chain of odd jobs. She had enough going that she wasn't overly reliant on any of them, and that's how she liked it. Mostly. Except for tonight, when Denver was being a frigid bitch.

She flexed her hands, trying to get the feeling back in them. After the first hour of her shift, her wool fingerless gloves were useless for anything except unlocking her phone. Still, she wouldn't trade her temporary discomfort for the security of not needing. It's better to be needed than to need. It took her years to learn that lesson. Years of hope and heartbreak and constant letdowns, but she'd learned it at last.

Darby's face flashed in her mind. She'd looked so perfect in the bed of the truck. Astrid wasn't sure why she hadn't just kissed her in the damn romantic falling snow. But there was an aura of goodness that surrounded Darby, like a protective force. And Astrid, well, she let people down. Sometimes when she meant to. But also sometimes when she tried her best not to. She needed low expectations. Whether she met them or flew miles above them was something time could work out.

Astrid rocked back on her stool until it balanced on two legs. She tipped her chin toward the night sky. Even in the city, the stars hung above her like shattered glass glittering on the street. A different sky hung over Colorado. In San Diego, she'd mostly seen low-flying planes and the occasional satellite. Here, the sky was lousy with stars she didn't recognize. She remembered watching the planes with her mom from their apartment balcony, always trying to determine if they were coming or going. But that movement, the possibility of change, was the constant in her life.

She should probably get back for a visit, but the thought of seeing her mom for the first time in two years sent a gridlock of guilt and anxiety through her. Best to leave that problem for future, wiser Astrid.

Something touched Astrid's shoulder, and she jumped. The stool pitched forward, making her stumble to her feet. She staggered a few steps as she caught her balance.

Astrid brought her palm to her chest, trying to contain her racing heart. She turned to see her friend standing with two steaming mugs. "You scared me, Hannah."

"No offense, but isn't it like your entire job to be alert?"

"Wow, straight for the jugular. I am alert, thank you very much. You snuck up on me."

"I said your name. Twice." Hannah handed one of the mugs to Astrid and shivered so violently that some of the liquid sloshed onto her boots.

"Fine. So I zoned out. It's not my fault no one wants to go out to a club in January."

"What were you thinking about all alone out here? The mysteries of the universe? Some babe you met?"

"A little of both, I guess." Astrid took a sip from the mug and grimaced. She'd definitely been hoping for whiskey, or at the very least something delicious. "What did you make me?"

"A virgin hot toddy because you're on the clock but also it's fucking freezing."

"So, hot water then? How come you get to drink on the clock but I just get sad water?"

"Because my job is pouring liquid into cups and your job is keeping us safe. We are not the same."

"No shit." Astrid took another drink and coughed as something abrasive hit the back of her throat. "Is that cayenne?"

"And lemon and honey. Let it heal what ails you, including your attitude tonight."

"I don't have an attitude. You don't have to stay out here for your entire break, you know."

"I know. But I want to. Working woman's solidarity and all that."

Astrid laughed. "I thought your phrase was 'you better work, butch'."

"It will be in five minutes. How'd your move go?"

"It was good, actually. Not much to report."

Hannah's blonde eyebrows rose until her gray beanie covered them. "Was that mild enthusiasm I just heard from Astrid West? Did you walk all your stuff over? You know I would have helped you."

"I ended up having help, actually."

"Oh, I'm glad you hired movers. I love you, but walking all your stuff to your new place in January made me question your sanity."

"So, this is going to sound weird."

"As opposed to every other conversation we've had?"

"Ok, fair. So, I met a girl the other night, and she offered to help me move."

"You met her where, here?"

"Yeah, she came for the speed dating thing."

"I've heard of u-hauling but moving as a first date is next level."

"It wasn't a date, at least I don't think it was. She might be the kindest person I've ever met. She helped me carry a mattress down the stairs of my building."

"Ok, so, an actual saint. Tell me about her."

"She came here with her friends and they own a house flipping company. She does the interior design for the properties."

"Wait, do you mean Darby? Messy brown curls, about my height, literal ray of sunshine?"

"You know her?"

"I've met her a few times. She helped me organize that birthday party last year. She's the best."

"Do you mean the one for your dog?"

"Yeah, it was perfect."

"That's the thing with Darby, I can't tell if she's just nice or if she's into me."

"No one would help you move a mattress if they didn't want to bang you on it. Or *be* banged on it. Or hopefully some sort of mutual banging arrangement."

"But she helped you organize an all-dog birthday party. So maybe she's just an equal opportunity generous person."

"She called it a Barkday. They all wore little bow ties made out of Milk Bones. I probably have pictures on my phone." Hannah laughed quietly with a dreamy look in her eyes. And Astrid tried to ignore the jealousy that was hollowing out her chest like a pumpkin.

"No need for that. I saw them on Buster's Instagram. It was very cute. But that's exactly what I mean. She swept me off my feet, but I can't tell if it was with romance or friendship."

"Hmm, okay. First, I'm so glad you follow Buster. Second, everyone loves dogs. No one likes moving mattresses. So tell me how you left it? Do you want to see her again?"

"I do. She said she had to go spend time with her friend's cat and that she'd call me. Which is usually a brush off, I know, but I think she meant it."

"Astrid. She showed up at your apartment early on New Year's Day and carried your shit. She'll definitely call. It's only been one day."

"Yeah, I'm sure you're right.

"Look, I've gotta get back. Don't freeze out here. And don't sulk. Try to just enjoy your Hot Toddy."

"This is a weak ass Hot Toddy. Enjoy your whiskey and your tips."

"You know I will. Come find me after your shift and I'll make you a real drink. And who knows, she might call any minute."

BUT DARBY DIDN'T CALL. The days ticked by and she didn't show up at Revel or at Astrid's new place to suddenly make her life better. A new feeling settled in Astrid's stomach, like she'd stepped into an emotional puddle and was stuck with wet socks. Inconvenient and annoying and impossible to ignore. She should have known better and dressed for the weather. But instead she was squelching through her days.

THE OCEAN IN A HANDBAG

DARBY

THE HOUSE HAD BEEN KEEPING DARBY BUSY, AND IT WAS NOT THE fun part of decorating. When she'd gone into business with James and Mia, she'd imagined artfully tossing moss green throw pillows onto vintage velvet couches. But changing the layout of a house included a stunning amount of math that she had to pretend to understand, while James patiently wrote it out in list form with her special flat pencil in her little notebook. Maybe Darby could get her some cute notebooks with their new company logo as a surprise.

Each new house project revealed another frustrating layer. It was like an onion in that it made her cry unless she simultaneously ate a lot of bread.

She'd spent most of the day trying to track down the Pinterest curtain Illuminati to figure out where to get the goods these days. Under no circumstances could they simply 'use the blinds that came with the place,' as James once suggested. She shuddered just thinking about it. Windows were the eyes to the house and curtains were the mascara. Not necessary, but the easiest way to elevate a look.

Between the curtains research and a flooring mix up, she

was several days late on her promise to reach out to Astrid. As she'd pinned pattern after pattern on her board, the thought of letting Astrid down had remained with her, like a computer update threatening to shut everything down if she kept ignoring it.

And that's why she was on this absolutely frigid street at quarter to midnight on a Wednesday with a date idea just this side of stalker-ish.

Astrid was sitting on her stool, just as Darby had been picturing her for the past five days. Her all-black outfit nearly blended with the night around her. Darby held her breath as Astrid rocked backward and blew a plume of steam into the night sky like a whale breaching the surface of the ocean. The ocean. That's why she was here. She patted her bag, feeling the weight of the gift she'd picked up earlier, and made her way over.

Darby waited as Astrid scrutinized the IDs of two women who were either eighteen or twenty-eight. That entire era had blurred once she'd turned thirty last year.

The women entered the bar and Astrid tipped back on her stool again nearly tumbling when she and Darby made eye contact.

"Hey, Jane Darby, you can just go in." Astrid gestured past her to the door of Revel.

"I'm happy to wait inside if you want. But I'm actually here to see you. I was wondering what time you're done with work?"

Astrid glanced at her watch. "Soon. Maybe fifteen minutes? Hannah will check IDs at the bar for the last few hours since it's so quiet tonight."

"That's great! If you don't have any plans after work, there's something I want to show you."

"It's kind of hard to make plans for midnight during the week."

Darby winked. "Is it? Well, I'll be inside. I guess I

shouldn't just assume you want to hang out with me, since I keep just showing up unexpectedly."

Astrid squinted at her. "So far you showing up unexpectedly hasn't been a bad thing. Unless you're here to collect on a bill, it's probably going to be the highlight of my day."

"Oh." Darby paused. She wasn't sure if Astrid was just being nice, but her compliment hit warm and bright in Darby's chest like a sip of hot chocolate. She tried to catch Astrid's eye, but she was staring at her boots. "Ok, great! Well, I'll see you in a bit."

Astrid nodded as she raised her gloved hands to her mouth to warm her fingers.

Darby paused, her hand braced on the door of the bar. "Are your hands cold?"

"Yeah, these gloves are pretty good, but by the end of my shift my body is determined to be cold."

"Here." Darby let go of the door and pulled off her knit mittens. She held them out toward Astrid, the cold air already nipping at her fingers. Astrid raised an eyebrow.

"Mittens, really?"

"Don't knock mittens. They're warmer than any gloves, I promise."

"Ok, I trust you." Astrid shed her gloves, stuffing them in her coat pocket, and pulled on the fair isle mittens.

The bright blue, green, and cream yarns were a striking contrast to Astrid's all-black ensemble. The effect was a bit Mickey Mouse, and Darby willed herself not to laugh. She bit her lip. "You look adorable."

"I feel like I'm about to pull a casserole out of the oven." Astrid grimaced as she turned her hands over.

"Exactly what I said, adorable!"

"I can't believe you found mittens with heart palm patches." Astrid studies the brown leather on the palms of the mittens.

"Oh, I didn't. I added those myself. It's nice to have a

grip and they're cute. James cut the leather hearts for me, but I think I'm not supposed to share that because Mia teased her for it." Darby chuckled. Another few women approached on the street, their voices echoing in the empty night. Darby gave Astrid a little wave and slipped inside the bar.

Darby was fishing the cherry out of her second Shirley Temple when Astrid sat down on the barstool next to her. The cold coming off of her felt like standing in front of an open freezer. A little shudder of sympathy ran through Darby's body as she turned to face her.

Astrid caught the bartender's attention with a smile. It was nice to think they might be friends. Astrid had struck Darby as staunchly independent, but she liked to be wrong. It was fun to be surprised by people. Humans are social creatures, even if they prefer to be alone or have had a lifetime of the world not giving them what they need, there was still something magical about being cared for.

Astrid set the mittens on the counter between them.

"So, what did you think?" Darby looked hopefully at Astrid.

"Of what?" A flash of confusion creased her brow, her dark eyebrows drawing together.

"Of the mittens, of course."

Astrid held up her hands in a gesture of surrender. "You were right. I'm now a mitten believer. Now I just need to find a pair of my own. Maybe I can order them."

"No way—I'll make you some!"

"Of course." Astrid laughed. "What did you have in mind for tonight?" Astrid's question interrupted Darby's musings.

"Ok, well, I hope this isn't weird, but I know it probably is weird. So promise to tell me if you hate it and we can totally do something else—whatever you want." The warmth of Astrid's hand on her arm stopped her runaway train of thought. Mittens really were better than gloves.

"It's getting a little weirder the longer you don't say it." Astrid's attempted wink took any sting out of her words.

"Hmm, maybe I should teach you how to wink instead… it's a good skill. An important skill."

"I'm very good at winking." Astrid gave it another attempt, both of her eyes narrowing and her mouth opening slightly.

Darby would have laughed at the sophomore effort if she hadn't been so busy looking at Astrid's mouth. One of her canine teeth was slightly angled. Darby had spent years in braces, and there were few things she found sexier than an imperfect smile—that kind of character could not be bought. She had a gap between her front teeth when she was younger and her mom had hated it, had stopped at nothing to eradicate it. She had the McMansion of smiles, but Astrid, Astrid had a Brooklyn Brownstone full of charm and potential.

"Are you going to tell me what this surprise is? Or should I guess?"

"Well, my original thought was a walk through downtown but I'm realizing now that might be the very last thing you want to do after a shift outside. Do you think it would be okay if we hang out here for a bit?"

"Absolutely, one time I even slept here. Sully treats us more or less like The Lost Boys—all are welcome, lots of food fights, etc."

"Sully owns the place?"

"Yeah."

Darby reached into her bag and pulled out the VR headset. Astrid raised an eyebrow but folded her hands in front of her, waiting patiently.

"Do you know what this is?"

"Some sort of video game?"

"Kind of. I feel like I should give you another caveat about how I can't help but pay attention to people but I think instead I'll hope this will seem charming."

Astrid raised one eyebrow. "Ok…"

"The other day when I was helping you move I noticed you didn't have a lot of stuff."

"Yeah, I kind of move a lot, so the less I have to pack, the better."

"Ok, we'll come back to that because having a beautiful space will change your life. Anyway, I noticed what you *did* have was pictures of the ocean. Like, a lot of them."

"Oh yeah, I love the ocean. When I was growing up my mom and I lived in San Diego for a while and the beach was my favorite place."

"Well, Denver's not exactly oceanfront," Darby said with a laugh. "And I think a road trip to the beach is a little out of season, but I thought maybe I could bring the ocean to you. I found this virtual reality thing that lets you swim in the ocean and explore the wildlife. You can pick the ocean and season or track migration patterns."

Astrid didn't say anything. Darby paused, she hovered between her desire to keep explaining and a nagging worry that this was the wrong thing. An overstep. It wouldn't be the first time. But how could something nice be the wrong thing? And Astrid had just said she liked the ocean.

Darby drew in a deep breath and pressed on. "So I guess I just thought maybe you would like it? Is it too nerdy? Too much? My friend Mia has found a hundred of the kindest ways to tell me that sometimes I'm a bit too much—"

Astrid caught Darby's hand as it arced through the air between them and laced their fingers together.

"No, it's um, really nice of you." Astrid paused and swallowed audibly, looking at their clasped hands. She slowly released her grip. "I can't believe you did this for me."

Darby watched Astrid fold her hands together on her lap. She would have held her hand all night but she didn't want to make Astrid uncomfortable. "You really like it? You'd tell me if you didn't, right?"

"Yeah, I'd tell you. I've never even heard of something like this. Where did you find it?"

"Last year we sold a house to the head researcher at the Denver Aquarium and she and I kept in touch—texts, holiday cards, the occasional movie night. That's not important. Anyway, it's something they use at her job to train new marine biology students. So I had to promise not to break it and also I think I'm babysitting every Friday night until summer."

"Wow, that's—I can't believe you did that for me." Astrid brushed a lock of jet black hair back from her face and it immediately fell back into her eyes.

"Sure, why not?" Darby shrugged. She could see the glimmer of moisture in Astrid's eyes and she glanced down to give her some privacy.

"Ok." Astrid cleared her throat. She reached for her mug and took a long drink. She grinned crookedly.

Darby wondered if she had imagined the way gratitude and sadness had fought in Astrid's dark brown eyes.

"Ready?"

Astrid looked apprehensive, but took another drink then nodded once decisively.

Darby leaned forward and guided the headset over Astrid's eyes, adjusting the back strap to make sure it was secure before she backed away slightly, though not all the way. She'd been thinking about Astrid nonstop since that morning they'd moved her mattress, but somehow this felt even more intimate than lying beside her.

The brush of Astrid's nose against her neck started her. "What do you smell like?"

Darby pinched the collar of her mauve sweater between her thumb and index finger. *Please don't be bad.* "Sawdust, probably. I've been over at the house a lot helping James with design decisions."

"No, it's good. Like something minty."

"Oh! That's chill vibes."

Astrid let out a laugh and then brought a hand to her mouth as though she needed to confirm that joy was hers. "Like how calm people smell?"

"It's an essential oil blend that Mia swears by. It's supposed to help you chill out, but I haven't been too stressed. I just like how it smells. Do you want to try some?"

"Sure." Astrid laughed again. "I'd love some of your chill vibes, Darby."

"Ok, it might be a little cold because it's been in my bag. Tilt your head to one side for me, please."

A slight smile played on Astrid's lips as she leaned to one side, exposing her neck. It was weird not being able to see her eyes to gauge her reaction. The headset made Astrid look a little like the Terminator. But the skin of her neck was warm and smooth, and deliciously alive beneath Darby's fingertips. She uncapped the glass vial and traced the rollerball in a small circle beneath Astrid's ear. Darby blew lightly on the spot to dry it, wondering what it would be like to lean forward a bit more. To close this distance between them.

Astrid shivered slightly as the oil made contact with her skin. "That's nice."

Darby's breath caught. She was glad Astrid hadn't taken off the headset, because it felt like the blush on her cheeks was as attention grabbing as a strobe light.

Chill, Darbs. She's probably just being nice. That was one of the pitfalls of being generally nice and upbeat, good moods could be infectious, like a really catchy song. It was hard to know sometimes if people were under the spell of her joy or simply playing along.

She smiled at Hannah and pointed at their drinks. Maybe something cold would help her chill out. She snuck a bit of the oil onto her wrist for good measure.

"Okay," she said leaning back and powering on the device. "Which ocean do you want?"

"Surprise me."

"Now *that* I can do."

Darby set the controls and watched as Astrid's mouth fell open, her tongue resting on her slightly crooked tooth. She ducked her head and let out a surprised yelp, swimming her hands in front of her, and shoved her goggles up.

"Are you alright?" Darby reached out and rested her hand on Astrid's knee trying to reassure her. "Did you see a shark?"

"I was surrounded by a bunch of penguins. They were diving around me and they kept getting so close." Astrid attempted to flatten her hair as she steadied herself. "I don't know why it startled me."

"Virtual reality can be unsettling. Do you want to stop?"

"No, I think I want to go back." Astrid slid the headset back down and let her hand fall on top of Darby's on her knee.

"Do you want the headphones?"

"No, I like having you here. Oh! The penguins are back." This time it was Astrid's laughter that filled the space between them.

"Oh, what kind?"

"The kind with bright orange beaks and the white around their eyes like a masquerade mask."

"Gentoo! I like those ones. So right now you're off the coast of Antarctica, but maybe next we could head somewhere warm?"

CHAPTER SIX

MEAT CUTE

ASTRID

THE NIGHT AIR WAS SHARP WHEN THEY EXITED THE BAR AN HOUR later. Astrid was unmoored, her legs unsteady like she'd just stepped off a ship and needed to relearn how to walk through this world. All the time she'd spent with Darby had felt like that, slightly isolated from reality; safe and floating.

Her night had begun with her sitting on a stool and ended with her swimming with loggerhead sea turtles just off the Florida Keys. Through it all had been the chime of Darby's laughter and the soft pressure of her hand on Astrid's knee. She'd placed it there when a Humpback whale had surfaced suddenly prompting Astrid to career out of her seat. Maybe Hannah was right—Darby had shown up to see her and the night had definitely been date-like. If Astrid played her cards right, the next few hours could be very date-like, too.

Darby's shoulder bumped against hers as they walked along the block. The lights of Revel blinked out behind them. Two hours ago she'd been desperate to get home and go to bed, and now Astrid was searching for reasons to prolong the night.

"Where are you parked?" Astrid scanned the empty street.

"I took a Lyft. I didn't plan on drinking, but just in case. Maybe I could walk you home and then call a car from there?"

The streetlights illuminated the constellation of freckles on Darby's nose. The dim lights of the bar had not done her justice. She had been beautiful in there, but out here she shone.

"Or I could just call one now. I don't mean to be presumptuous, I know you've had a long day, and I already made it a bit longer." Darby had her phone in her hand before Astrid realized she still hadn't responded.

"Sorry, still thinking about the ocean." Astrid needed to get it together. This is what she was hoping for—Darby wanted to go home with her. A vision of the two of them eating waffles tomorrow morning wafted through Astrid's mind. She really needed to find a place that delivered breakfast. "I'd love to walk together."

Instead of responding, Darby did a little hop step and linked her arm through Astrid's. In her chest, Astrid's heart did an answering leap as she turned them toward her apartment.

THEY LINGERED outside of the banged-up wooden door of Astrid's apartment building while Astrid looked at her boots, trying to think of a way to invite Darby up. A way that would result in the absolute least amount of embarrassment if she declined.

She hated these awkward early moments. Tonight had felt like something, a spark. Maybe more than a spark. The entire world lit up around Darby. At Revel, Hannah had checked on Darby, then lingered. She had a brightness that drew people in like moths. It was like no one wanted their time with her to end. So maybe this was nothing. But maybe it was something.

And the chance of something was more than Astrid had looked forward to in a while.

Astrid had a feeling that if anyone could decline an advance and leave you feeling good about yourself, it was Darby. She straightened her shoulders and looked into Darby's hazel eyes—green in the center, surrounded by a circle of deep brown that made Astrid think of moss-covered trees. "Would you want to come up—"

"This door would be really cute painted mint green."

Their laughter overlapped.

"Sorry, go ahead." Astrid shoved her hands into her pockets and ducked her head. Her fingers were numb without Darby's mittens. She'd been tempted to keep them. She wasn't joking about the mittens being incredibly warm, but she'd gallantly slid them back across the bar. She probably couldn't pull off mittens with hearts anyway.

A truck tore down the street, bass rattling the windows of her building. The music flashed like a siren, loud enough to rival five-minutes-to-midnight-on-NYE loud. Astrid's mind flashed to desperate club dancing. Warm bodies pressed close. Her eyes fell to Darby's mouth. Shoot, she was still talking. Astrid tuned back in.

"Anyway, a unique door can add a lot of curb appeal. Plus, you know, it's cute."

"I'm not sure I can paint the building door. What color is your door?"

"It's mustard yellow, and the house is slate gray with a deep blue undertone. I've been thinking about repainting it though, something more cheerful."

"There are colors more cheerful than yellow?"

"Sure, any color can be cheerful if it makes you happy."

"Oh. That's a really nice thought, actually. I've been thinking that I'd love a way to pay you back for helping me move."

"There's no need to pay me back. I wanted to be there."

"Ok, well maybe I could be there for you sometime?"

Darby tilted her head to the side and squinted one eye closed. "What are you doing Tuesday? And how do you feel about painting?"

"Nothing and neutral, I guess."

"Perfect."

Above them the street light shuddered out, throwing them into the darkness like a play between acts. The telltale brush of a cat's tail swiped behind Astrid's knees.

When the light flickered back on Darby was squatting down and struggling to lift a giant orange cat that promptly flopped onto its back and batted at her hair. A wave of relief rushed through Astrid. Meatball hadn't been around much since she'd moved and it was weird eating her meals uninterrupted by his paw swatting her fork to the floor.

"Ah, well, now you've met Meatball."

"Nice to meet you, Meatball." Darby laughed. "I guess this is a meat cute."

Astrid gave the pair a puzzled look. "A meet what?"

"You know, like in a rom-com when the characters' paths cross and they, like, crash into each other and ruin each other's lives for one act. That's called a meet cute. But this is a m-e-a-t cute because of his name."

Astrid understood about two percent of that but nodded anyway. "He's kind of naughty, but I love him."

"What happened to his ear? Did he get hurt?" Darby ran her fingers gently over the ragged edge of Meatball's left ear, most of which was missing.

"I'm not sure. He came like that."

"Is he your cat?"

"No, he's a cat I take care of."

Darby tilted her head to the side and Meatball, who she was now cradling, craned his neck like an owl and followed suit.

"He showed up one day at my last apartment. He was just

passed out on the couch when I got home, covered in pasta sauce from the dinner I'd made before work. I took him to the vet to make sure he was healthy and he's been around ever since. I'm sure the food and catnip I get him doesn't hurt either. Now he mostly follows me into the building at night and back out in the morning."

"Got it. So he's an indoor/outdoor cat. Did you move him with you? I don't remember seeing him in your apartment."

Meatball burrowed his nose against Darby's neck. Astrid had never realized she could feel jealous of a cat. Meatball paused and made direct, taunting eye contact with her.

"He's not mine to move. I mean he did do the walk with me to this new place a few times. But he was out and about for the big move. I actually haven't seen him much the past few days." Astrid's mind flashed to the posters she'd been thinking of drawing and the few sketches of Meatball she'd practiced.

"Wise boy. Moving is a beast and unpacking isn't much better." Darby scratched under Meatball's chin and when his jade green eye caught Astrid's gaze, he gave her the cat equivalent of a shit-eating grin. Don't bite the hand that feeds you, but she supposed there wasn't a saying about not stealing the hand's girlfriend.

Whoa, not girlfriend. A friend who's a girl. A woman. Gal who's a pal. Astrid begged her mind to be quiet.

Headlights down the street slowly approached and Astrid took a few steps forward until she was angled between Darby and the street. Meatball swatted at her, his paw anchoring in her coat and yanking her back like she was a fish he'd caught. If this cat ripped her only warm coat she would… well, she'd probably do nothing at all, because what could she do, really. He was the definition of incorrigible.

Cars driving slowly always gave her an eerie feeling, like they were definitely going to kidnap her. That or they were texting.

Darby leaned past her and waved to the car who sped up to careen toward them then slammed to a stop along the curb.

"Well, this is me. I'll send you the address for Monday, but really no pressure to come help paint."

"Oh right, of course." As Astrid's adrenaline from the near-kidnapping faded, feelings of foolishness and disappointment swirled in her gut like a terrible mixed drink which was regretted the moment it was imbibed. "I didn't realize you'd called a car."

"Yeah, I just figured it's pretty late and you're probably tired after work?"

Once Darby mentioned it, she was exhausted. The kind of pure tiredness that hours in the cold gave her. "Totally, well, I'll let you go. Text me when you make it home?"

Darby grinned. "I'd love to! I mean, of course." She leaned in and wrapped her arms around Astrid's shoulders.

Astrid let her arms fall around Darby's waist. And the only thing unsettling about it was how natural it felt. She breathed in Darby's minty scent, while Meatball dug his claws into the thigh of her jeans and tried to do a pull-up.

"Goodnight!" Darby placed a quick kiss on Astrid's cheek, so fast she wasn't sure it happened, and the next thing she knew Darby was sliding into the back seat of the sedan.

Meatball made a break for it and lept after her. Darby's laugh emanated from the darkness of the car's interior. "I know buddy, I'll miss you too."

She set Meatball back on the sidewalk and Astrid quickly scooped him up before he could attempt another stowaway. "Trust me, buddy. I don't want her to go either."

The two of them watched the car until the tail lights flashed at the corner, then disappeared.

Astrid had brought her fair share of women home from Revel over the past year, but never quite like that.

CHAPTER SEVEN

THE PASTRY CURE

DARBY

DARBY BACKED OUT OF HER DRIVEWAY AND WAVED TO DR. Sylveria as the old woman shuffled down the walkway to collect her morning paper. Her bare legs peeked out beneath her pink robe, and Darby gave a sympathetic shiver.

"Hey, Siri"

"I'm listening."

"Please set a daily reminder for eight a.m. for me to bring Dr. Sylveria's newspaper to her porch for her."

"Ok, your daily reminder is set for eight a.m."

"Thank you! Can you also play Holy Ground by Taylor Swift?"

She took the turn out of her neighborhood and headed downtown as she and Taylor sang about spinning in a brand new dress.

The January sun was shining brightly, and Darby had somehow talked Mia into blowing off emails and joining her for an early lunch. Two minor miracles and it was only eleven a.m.

Darby slipped on her heart-shaped sunglasses and they

bathed the streets of downtown Denver in their rose-colored hue. This was her absolute favorite way to view the world.

The buildings grew gradually taller as she neared the city center, like flowers in the spring rising from the earth. She didn't go to the Flippin' Fantastic office much. Mia had things covered and Darby found the atmosphere a bit uptight in that both singing and dancing were frowned upon. Something about clients and professionalism. It wasn't important.

The ring of her phone through the car stereo cut through her music, really messing up her vibe. She switched lanes and tapped the answer button on the dashboard touch screen. Mia loved to get an accurate ETA.

"This is Darby. I will see you in ten minutes and then we're going to eat so many chocolate croissants you will need a full week to recover," she said in her best important-business-woman voice.

"Hello, Jane. I really wish you'd stop going by that name."

If her good mood was a balloon her mother was sharp as a tack. "Oh, hi, Mom. I didn't realize it was you."

"Yes, clearly."

"What can I do for you?"

"Your father and I wanted to see how your business is doing."

"Oh." Darby took a minute to process her mother calling to ask about her life. It was... unexpected. "It's really great actually. We just bought this amazing property that we're renovating. Well, Mia found it, actually. And of course, James is handling anything that has to do with power tools. I've got a really good feeling about this one. Like we're finally hitting our stride."

"That's nice, dear. Listen, your father and I were talking with Alan Greer the other night. You remember Alan, of course. He and your father taught in the Economics department together when you were in middle school. He wrote that paper on the behavioral economics of the melting ice caps."

Was her mother under the impression that she followed behavioral economics research? "Um, I'm not—"

"Well, we ran into him at a lecture and it turns out he's got an in with the board at UConn. Have you thought any more about going back to school?"

"I, um, I've been pretty busy running a business. You know, putting my Master's degree to work."

"A design degree from an artsy hippie school is hardly a Master's."

"Huh, someone should tell that to my diploma."

"Honey, you know we're proud of you. But it's hard to see you waste your potential. You could be brilliant if you just tried a little harder. And you don't have to go where your father and I teach. Getting your doctorate from a state school is very respectable. It's time to stop focusing on fun and think seriously about your future."

"I co-founded a successful company and I get to work with my best friends every day. That's my definition of success."

"I'm glad you're enjoying yourself, Jane, but what happens when the market crashes? Sure, spending time with your friends and decorating houses is fun, but what about your future? I know you care about Mia and James, Jane, and of course, you don't want to let them down; but you have to understand that your father and I just want you to do something worthwhile."

"Caring for people is worthwhile."

"Of course it is. Look, I have to get to class. Just look at the application I emailed you. I filled out everything I could. And don't worry too much about your CV or transcript. We can get you in."

The line went silent and Darby let her head bang against

the headrest and drew in a deep breath once and then again before she reached forward and turned the music back up.

Croissants were in her future and in her experience there was very little in this world that couldn't be fixed with flaky pastry.

"OH, NO, WHAT'S WRONG?"

Darby glanced up at Mia where she'd stopped short in the doorway to her office. Concern creasing the space between her perfect brows.

The office had been empty when Darby arrived so she'd made herself at home by lying on the plush white rug covering the floor. She'd kicked her legs up on the couch in front of her.

A small pink package flew over Mia's shoulder and landed on Darby's stomach.

"Thanks, Arty, I'm promoting you from assistant to lifesaver."

Darby unwrapped a piece of bubble gum and popped it in her mouth.

"I can't believe you have our PA running out to get you bubble gum."

"I didn't. He keeps a stash in his desk next to the other necessities like aspirin and tampons."

"Arty has tampons in his desk… for us?"

"Well, you don't have to use them, but he's a good man in a storm. I see you're wearing pantyhose? Like an actual superhero."

"Yes, Darbs. I'm wearing business attire at our place of business. You don't get to change the subject that easily when you don't have a poker face. Something's off."

"Nothing's wrong. I'm thinking about breakfast."

Mia tugged down the edges of her pencil skirt and lowered herself to the floor in slow motion. "Nuh-uh. I'd know this position anywhere. So who do I need to beat up? Your mom or your dad?"

"It was my mom. She's back on her a-PhD-is-the-only-way-to-give-my-life-meaning campaign."

"So hurricane Debs rocked your morning. But you know what?"

A laugh bubbled up from Darby's throat. "God, she hates when we call her Debs."

"Precisely. But you, my lovely friend, are 2,000 miles and two time zones away. You can call her Debs every day of the week."

"That's a very good point."

Mia's fingertips brushed Darby's forehead as she slid her sunglasses onto her hair. Darby squinted against the harsh reality of the fluorescents.

"You know, I'm really digging these overalls, but I thought we were going out to eat."

Darby glanced down at her paint-covered denim ensemble. "Huh. And you think people will mind?"

"You know what Darbs, I think they'll probably love you anyway."

"WHAT WAS THAT?" Mia leveled Darby with her best business stare. The one that always made Darby sit up straight and spit out her gum.

Darby gulped down the bite of chocolate croissant she'd been chewing and maybe, possibly, trying to talk around. "So what's the deal with you and Lauryn?"

"You mean our client, Ms. Sucre? There's no deal. I'm trying to find her a house, same as every other person who walks through our office doors." Mia nodded at the waiter as he set down her espresso and Darby's hot chocolate.

"No, I mean Lauryn Sucre, the woman behind your great heartbreak who just happens to be a client. Did you want me to step in and work with her? I could show her some houses."

"I appreciate your support, Darbs, I do, but there's a lot more to my job than just unlocking doors."

"I know that."

"Ugh, I'm sorry. Of course, you do. I know you're trying to help. I'm just stressed and this whole having to work with my enemy thing is bringing up a lot of unpleasant memories."

"Is she your enemy though? Weren't you both sort of wronged in that situation?"

"Darby, for two seconds, I need you to stop giving everyone the benefit of the doubt."

"Ok, got it." Darby closed her eyes and took a deep breath. She tried to channel her mother's hard-line practicality. "Do we really need the money that badly? How big of a boost can one person really give to the business? Can you refer her to someone else?"

"It's bad business to hand a competitor a client like Lauryn. She's a successful musician and she's friends with our other big-name clients. So I'm thinking about this as an investment in the future of our company."

"That's a lot of pressure for you to take on. Is there anything I can do?"

"You can tell me if you hooked up with the bouncer from the other night yet."

Darby sputtered, choking on a sip of hot chocolate. "Mia Stone! You know I'm not the kind of gal who would kiss and tell." Though she had been kicking herself for not kissing Astrid goodnight. *Really* kissing her anyway.

"Does that mean there's nothing to tell?"

"That is so not the point. I like Astrid. I'm enjoying getting to know her."

"So that's a no. I love you, Darbs, but maybe it's time for you to take a chance with your heart. Have a little fun."

"I have fun all the time. We're having fun right now."

"No, babe, we're eating pastries."

CHAPTER EIGHT

HALF OKAY

ASTRID

Astrid toyed with the pull of her leather jacket. She loved the racket the old metal made, like gnashing teeth. She wasn't sure how seriously she was supposed to take Darby's intention to paint. When she'd gotten dressed, she might have been secretly hoping that this was more of a date and less a day of hard labor. Though she'd dig a trench for six hours if it meant she got to spend those six hours next to Darby. She'd probably be adorable with a smear of dirt on her cheek.

Ok enough. Today was the day she was going to kiss Jane Darby. The thought sent warmth through her body. Astrid knew she'd blown her chance on her doorstep the other night, with an assist from Meatball, of course. But today she had a plan. For starters, she looked great. Not a speck of Meatball fur on her outfit, basically the eighth wonder of the world when you wore as much black as Astrid did and had a giant orange cat squatting in your apartment like it was a McDonald's near a high school.

Astrid respected Meatball's hustle, finding free shelter and warm meals while remaining a free agent. If only she could get him to stop bringing her nightmare presents of street meat. What was she doing thinking about her cat when she had the nicest woman in the world to charm? Darby treated her like she had something to offer and for once she wanted to give freely.

She double-checked the house number and started up the path. This was definitely the place Darby told her they were flipping. Even if she didn't have the address, it was the only bright yellow front door on the block.

And if that wasn't a giveaway, the most Jane Darby car she'd ever seen was parked out front—tiny and an aggressively cheerful red. The back windshield sported an actual rainbow. Not some understated LGBTQIA flag decal, but an arching rainbow swooped across one corner of the glass and ended in big fluffy clouds. It looked like something that belonged on the stomach of a Care Bear. She smiled at it despite herself.

A woman who looked vaguely familiar milled about in the front yard one house over. Were Darby and her friends working on that house too? Astrid nodded at the woman and she had spun so fast to avoid a hello that her dark bob haircut flared over her shoulders like the skirt of a flapper's dress. Okay, maybe not one of Darby's friends then.

The woman crouched down and pulled the branch of one of her hedges close to her face like she was looking for clues. A weird activity for a frigid January morning, but then again, Astrid had never lived in a house. Maybe hedges required constant vigilance.

In front of Astrid, the bright yellow front door flew open and Darby leaned against the door frame. Her paint-splattered overalls were unhooked on one side, displaying a bit of her abdomen where her cropped white t-shirt ended. It wasn't until the cold air hit Astrid's molars that she realized her mouth had dropped open. Darby ran a hand through her messy hair and cocked her head to one side. She had a streak of paint on her nose; Astrid was done for.

"Hey, Astrid! Is that what you're wearing?"

Astrid looked down at her black jeans and boots. Beneath her leather jacket was a black t-shirt. Honestly, one of her favorite outfits. "It would appear so," she said with a smirk. "Is that what you're wearing?"

"Of course!" Darby gestured up and down her overalls, drops of paint making them look somewhere between drop cloth and a Pollock knock off. "This is my painting ensemble. I've worn them at every house we've worked on, sort of like a little renovation scrapbook! Anyway, we can get into that later. I'm worried you're going to ruin your clothes and we don't want that. I think I have an extra shirt in my car at least, and maybe James has coveralls or something."

"Oh, no, that's okay—" She'd selected this outfit. No way was she going to be dressed like some thrift store Barbie. She was trying to *impress* Darby.

But Darby was halfway down the walk, moving with joy and urgency that were in no way called for.

"You can head in! James is taping off the walls." Darby called out.

Astrid grimaced at the thought of spending the day with James, too. She seemed nice enough if a little quiet, but in her experience, it was very hard to flirt with a woman in front of her friends.

"Oh, one more thing—be careful with the door, the marigold paint is still a little tacky."

"I don't think it's tacky, it looks nice."

"I meant to the touch, silly." Darby's head and shoulders disappeared into the backseat of her car where she rummaged.

Astrid had to admit, the overalls were kind of perfect.

"Trust me, just put them on."

Astrid looked between the atrocity of the clothes in her

hand and Darby who was smiling at her like she'd saved the day. She knew she couldn't say no, not when Darby was looking at her like that.

"Ok, sure, thanks for thinking of my clothes."

"I mean they look great on you." Darby's eyes trailed down Astrid's body in a spark of electricity that she felt down to her toes. "And I just want to make sure they stay that way! The coveralls might be a little bit big because they're for James the giant but I think they'll work. You can just cuff the legs."

"Perfect."

In the half torn up bathroom Astrid pulled off her clothes and slipped on the coveralls up to her waist, knotting the arms securely around her hips. She slipped the baseball tee over her head and was alarmed when it stopped just below her ribs. The edge was a little uneven. Someone had cropped this top *intentionally*. What kind of perso—

"Everything okay in there?" Darby's called.

"It's half okay." Astrid wrestled with the hem of the shirt, but no amount of tugging made this thing cover her belly button. "Um, Darby, where's the rest of this shirt?"

"Oh, that's a funny story. I was wearing it at the CRJ concert and James spilled her vodka lemonade on it, so we cut the stained part on the bottom with her pocket knife. I'm still not clear on how she got a pocket knife into the concert."

"How bad was the lemonade stain? Isn't that, like, almost clear?"

"James only likes pink lemonade. Don't tell her I told you that. It's a secret, I think. Like I'm not sworn to secrecy per se but it's been heavily implied through looks and sighs and an icy silence when I mentioned it to Mia one time."

That was an incredible amount of information and Astrid found herself at a loss for words. She looked at her reflection. The three quarter-length red sleeves were somehow longer than the shirt itself. The front said "It's Not Christmas Till

Somebody Cries" surrounded by stars. She felt like she was about to star in a gritty 80s movie about a woman with a dream to perform. She looked down at her stomach. This look was really putting the flash in Flashdance.

Astrid might not love it, but at least the crop top showed off the sexy tattoo on her side. Monster tattoos were sexy, right?

Astrid let out a sigh with the strength of a stage fan. Her hair blew up and landed back in her eyes. She turned on the tap to throw some water on it before Darby offered her a headband or something.

She eased open the bathroom door and was met with a squeal of delight. At least pleasing Darby had a nice ring to it.

"You're spectacularly bad at that, you know," Darby said with a laugh.

Had Astrid ever been insulted in a way that felt like a compliment before?

Astrid looked at the wall in front of her. The uneven streaks of gray paint from the roller looked a little like barbed wire. She'd been nervous to over commit with too much paint. "Did I forget to mention I've never painted before?"

Astrid turned to look at Darby. Her shoulders tensed as she braced herself for some flash of judgment in those green eyes; but instead, there was an unmistakably mischievous smile pulled up one corner of her mouth. Darby's hand reached for hers and stilled the roller. She looked at the wall like it was an adorable drawing from a favorite niece a monstrous princess—all purples and greens. Like it was terrible but also that was part of why she loved it; part of its charm.

"I maybe forgot to ask." Darby winked and Astrid thought back to the bar and the way Darby had of teasing her in such a way that it pulled her in rather than pushed her away. Darby seemed to use teasing like a love language. *Like she cared about you enough to give you a hard time*, Astrid thought.

"But that's okay it's just the first coat."

"We have to do this more than once?"

"Did you not paint your room growing up? When I was nine I saved my brownie sales money and bought a gallon of bubble gum pink paint for my room."

"That feels right. My mom and I always lived in apartments and we couldn't afford to lose our security deposit. Plus, we moved a lot."

"Oh, that totally makes sense. I did a terrible job with that pink paint anyway. It was like Mr. Bubbles exploded. But what about now that you rent your own place?"

"I mostly find places that are month-to-month. I don't like to stay anywhere for too long. You probably noticed I don't have much furniture. Too much stuff weighs me down like I'm underwater and can't reach the surface." Astrid's mouth hung open for a few seconds, she struggled to make sense of sharing so much with Darby.

"I can understand that in theory. But don't you think you could use some furniture, like at least a shelf for your books? It could be so cute."

"I will tentatively consider one shelf."

"Say no more." Darby pulled out her phone and frantically tapped something into it. "Just setting a reminder for something."

"I don't want to spend a lot of energy on making my place nice. I've already been in Denver for a year, so I'm reaching my term limit."

Something moved across Darby's face like a cloud covering the sun, but a moment later it was gone.

"Why would you leave Denver? It's the best! I'm here. And Revel. And Meatball. Plus, making places cute is kind of my whole thing." Darby gave her a charming smile.

Astrid laughed and shuffled her feet. A light gust of air from the fan across the room raised goosebumps on her bare stomach. In what world was she having a serious discussion with a woman she was interested in while wearing a belly shirt? "I can't stay for just one person, even if you are the best. The city has to charm me and I just haven't fallen in love with it, I guess. And if I was going to, I probably would have by now, right? I figure the right city for me is out there somewhere—the place where I will feel magically at home. I just have to find it and once I do everything will fall into place."

"Fine."

"Fine, what?"

"Challenge accepted."

"There was no challenge, Darby."

"As a goodwill ambassador for the city of Denver in the great state of Colorado, get ready to be charmed. Please clear your schedule for Friday afternoon because you're about to get a mile high on love."

"Wow, that was terrible, but let's see what you've got, I guess."

ALL AFTERNOON JAMES had been doing drive bys. She would peer over Astrid's shoulder, her light eyes sending criticisms she'd never actually utter if their interactions so far were anything to go by. She'd just wandered back in to "re-check on the color of the tile grout with Darby."

Astrid felt very much like she was being chaperoned and one errant brush stroke would disqualify her as a potential suitor for Darby. Though maybe she should disqualify herself if she wasn't planning on staying in Denver. Darby hadn't mentioned looking for a commitment, but she seemed like the type of woman that you wouldn't want to let go. And Astrid had built a life by surrounding herself with things that were easy to let go.

The fabric of her pants rustled as James was crouched low to inspect the trim for any drops of paint. She scrubbed at one Astrid couldn't see with a wet rag. Astrid had to admire her dedication to a house they weren't even keeping.

THE FRONT DOOR suddenly banged open, causing all three of them to jump.

"Wow, you two are still painting this room? Are you finger painting the walls, Darbs? Is this a new trend?" Mia shouldered the front door closed. She cradled a cardboard drinks tray in her hand filled with four identical red and white cups. "I brought everyone a Darby Special for fortifications."

A chorus of "Yes" and "Thank God" from Darby and James nearly drowned out Astrid's question.

"What's a Darby Special?"

"A peanut butter milkshake topped with marshmallow fluff and sprinkles." Mia looked at her like she was explaining basic math.

"Oh okay." That sounded absolutely sweet enough to make Astrid sick, but it was nice of Mia to bring her one.

Mia cheers-ed them and Astrid took a tentative sip and then another. This cup was filled with what might actually be heaven. Okay, so, maybe Mia showing up wasn't the absolute worst thing that could have happened, even if she did now have two of Darby's friends watching her every move.

"I can't believe you don't have any music on in here, Darbs." Mia walked over to the lavender Bluetooth speaker and powered it on. A moment later the room sounded like a middle school dance. If the wall wasn't wet Astrid would have glued herself to it.

Darby and Mia danced together in the center of the room, a dropcloth bunching beneath their feet. Mia was completely put together in a black skirt and emerald green blouse; her heels reminded Astrid of ice picks as they struck the floor.

James knelt and secured to corners of the cloth to the floor with blue tape.

James took a few steps backward, retreating to the corner. Her head bopped while her body remained still. She imagined herself looking uncannily like a bobblehead in a slow-moving car.

"Come on, Astrid, dance with us!" Darby reached out her hand at the same moment Astrid stepped forward. Darby's movements were magnetic, and she was dressed for a dance interlude, after all. Darby's fingertips, with their slightly chipped purple polish, landed on Astrid's bare hip, just above the knotted coveralls.

Astrid let herself be pulled forward, anything to prolong that feeling of Darby's touch on her bare skin. Darby's touch was delicate but steady. Like she was going to get what she wanted, but she'd be nice about it.

Astrid stepped close and swayed against her. When her mouth got close to Darby's ear she glanced to where James was now standing in the corner. She was looking at Astrid and Darby like she was contemplating pulling out her ruler to enforce a six-inch distance between their swaying bodies.

"How come James doesn't have to dance?"

Darby followed Astrid's gaze to the corner. "That is James dancing."

CHAPTER NINE

DAMN GOOD FRIES

DARBY

She bounced up and down on the vinyl seat of the booth a few times, enjoying the creak and give of the old material.

"Darby, I love you, but we were just here like two days ago. If we keep up this pace I'm going to have to go back to spin class."

"Number one, you're a model to me no matter what size you wear. And number two, when we were here before it was for a James intervention."

"Oh, shit," Mia muttered under her breath as she slid in across from her friend.

"Do not worry, no one's getting interventioned today."

"Not sure that's a word," James said as she pulled off her beanie and set it on the table.

"Ok, except for maybe James again for being the vocabulary police."

"Please don't, I can't take another intervention. You already have me leaving work when the sun goes down like a farmer."

"Well, that just makes good sense. There's more to life than just nailing things."

Mia looked at her like she was holding back a sneeze and the next thing she knew she was laughing so hard water was streaming from her eyes. "Damn Darbs." She ran a finger under her lashes to tidy her eyeliner. "You've gotta warn a gal before you make a James sex joke."

"I didn—Ohh, nailing things like boards or whatever, not the binocular lady next door. Unless James has something she'd like to share."

James' face went so red she started to blend into the booth. "Don't you have something to share, Darbara?"

"I do, but let's order first. That way if you don't like it you won't leave because fries are imminent."

"Ok spill." Mia gestured to Darby with a crinkle-cut fry before dipping it in a mixture of mayonnaise and ketchup.

"Ok, I honestly think if you open yourselves up you'll be very excited about this idea. But before you say no, it's important to remember that I've already bought all the food, including your favorites."

"Oh, that's cold," Mia said, turning to James. "Did you know she had that in her?"

"It's absolutely arctic. Now when you say favorites, do you mean…"

"Pink lemonade, peanut butter pretzels, everything for loaded nachos. The works."

"Consider my mind open."

"Great! That's one." Darby grinned and turned her attention to Mia.

Mia pushed her plate of fries away from her and folded her hands on the table, her light polish immaculate on her short nails. "I'm ready to hear your proposal, but I'll withhold judgment until the brand of pretzels is confirmed."

"Maybe you'll just have to show up on Sunday to see. I was thinking of having a get-together."

"Like more than the three of us, you mean?"

"Yeah, but only a few more. I figured with Denver in the Super Bowl it might be fun."

"Since when do you care about the Super Bowl?"

"Since I found out about the snacks."

DARBY LINED up the final b in Jagerbomb on the Super Bowl jersey she was making for James. She'd draped Mia's sunshine jersey over her clothes rack so the ink could dry. When she'd tried to scrub the blue paint from her hands earlier, they'd gone the shade of cookie monster. There were definitely worse colors to be than blue.

Her phone screen lit up with a call from her fruit baskets group chat. It was a cute name for the three of them plus a fun way to troll James, which also felt important.

"Hey, babes." She singsonged.

"Hey Darbs," Mia said. She looked flawless even though Darby was pretty sure the top she was seeing was part of a pajama set. And the lighting—had she bought a ring light for her phone?

A moment later James' face popped into view, her short hair erratic as a wheat field at threshing time. "Hello?" James always seemed bewildered by impromptu video calls, though by now she'd had years of practice.

"Hey, Jager—"

"Darbara, please stop trying to make Jagerbomb a thing."

"I'm pretty sure you made it a thing when you started introducing yourself that way to pretty women in bars." Mia smirked.

James sighed; a moment later they watched her do a trust fall onto her couch. That couch had been one of Darby's better finds when she was helping James decorate.

"Let's get down to the important matters. Why are your hands blue, Darbs?"

Darby wiggled her fingers at the phone's camera. "Just trying out a new craft project."

"That's cool." James lifted her head off the couch pillow. "Will we get to see it?"

"You will absolutely get to see it very soon."

"Great." Mia nodded. "So, I need to talk to you about Lauryn."

"I still can't believe you're making it with a rockstar." James shifted on the couch. Maybe they needed to find her more comfortable throw pillows.

"No one says making it anymore, Jagerbomb."

"Do not make me accidentally drop my phone in my coffee, Mia."

Darby laughed at James' serious face that made her look uncannily like an angry Berenstain Bear. "Yeah, James, it's called smashing now."

Mia rolled her eyes. "We're not calling it either of those. Anyway, as I was trying to say, you know how my brother had an emergency last week and Lauryn helped me get my niece and nephew from school and the little traitors fell instantly in love?"

"Yup!" Darby nodded as she finished up James' jersey.

"A tabloid got a picture."

"Wait, what? I don't think paparazzi exist in Colorado."

"Have camera, will travel," James said.

"Right, I forgot about planes." Darby grimaced. "Are they going to run it?"

Darby's phone chimed at a text from Mia with a link to LA Now.

"Oh, shit," James said. "Did Cori call you?"

"Only like twenty times to interrogate me about why I'm seeking revenge on her with the celebrity who caused the break up of our engagement."

Darby tried to catch Mia's eye, but she was looking off to the side. "I mean, a lot of things broke off your engagement, right? A viral photo of Cori kissing Lauryn at a part was just one of them."

"I know and I've tried explaining that my life and the things happening in it are no longer about her."

"Here, here!" James raised her coffee mug with her cat's face on it in a little salute.

"But she called when Lauryn was here after we, you know—"

"Smashed." Darby nodded.

"Made it." James seconded.

"I think it's over before it really got started." Mia let out a deep sigh that was very close to a sob.

"No way." Darby caught her eye this time. Tears gathered like dew on Mia's lashes, and Darby's own eyes glossed over in response. "I've seen the way she looks at you. She looks at you like you're the home she wants in Denver. I mean, she's buying a house from you after seeing it for five minutes. She's into Mia. Right, James?"

James' amber eyes went wide like she'd just been called on in class while doodling. "Right."

"Ok, enough about me." Mia blinked rapidly. "Tell us more about Astrid. You two seemed pretty cozy painting at the house the other day."

"I always want to hear more about you, but okay." Mia swiped at her eyes. Darby would throw her a lifeline. "I really like her!"

"And she likes you too, literally no one else would wear your Carly Rae Jepsen belly shirt." James laughed.

"Be careful or that's what you're getting for Christmas," Mia said through a watery laugh. "I think she's serious about you, Darbs, and not just because of the shirt thing."

"Yeah." Darby nodded thoughtfully. "I mean, I'm not naïve—I know a lot of people humor me, and they think that because I'm happy I must not be very smart. Or they imagine that maybe my life has been too easy to understand what they've gone through. Or are still going through. But Astrid looks at me like she sees me."

"We see you, too, Darbs," James said

"I know that. But Astrid also looks at me like she wants to see me naked."

"Yeah, that's a difference," Mia said.

"I mean no offense." James' face was taking on the hue of pink lemonade. "It's just that—"

"Wait." Mia cut in. The relief at being interrupted was plain on James' face.

"Yeah?" Darby sat down on the floor readying herself for the Mia question special. She really would have made a great investigative reporter.

"Has Astrid seen you naked?" Mia furrowed her brow.

"Well, no, not yet. At least I hope it's not yet and not just no." Darby would give money to make herself stop talking.

"Okay, good. I was about to be very hurt if that happened and you didn't call us immediately," Mia said.

"Women don't react well when I call you two right after sex."

"Well, that's on them."

CHAPTER TEN

A SHELF TO BUILD A DREAM ON

ASTRID

ONCE AGAIN HAVING BASICALLY ZERO POSSESSIONS WAS REALLY paying off. Darby would be here any minute with "the best surprise" and Astrid's apartment was spotless. Well, if you didn't count the giant orange spot directly in the middle of the entryway. Meatball yawned and rolled over as if Astrid's thoughts had disturbed him.

A knock sounded on her door. Astrid held her breath as she waited for it to end but it continued on, like when someone makes their ringtone an entire song then listens to it rather than answering. Where did she know that beat from? *Darby.*

Even her knocks were cheerful enough to make Astrid smile. She was in deep trouble.

"Excuse me, I'm here to see a-Mister Meatball," Darby called from the other side of the door. Her Mario impression drew a bark of laughter from Astrid she'd never heard herself make before.

She hopped over Meatball and he swiped at her leg, his claws a Venus flytrap that snapped into the ankle of her black jeans. She hopped the last few inches pulling him along with her as she reached for the door.

Darby's dark messy hair sprung out from beneath her beanie. It was a blue Broncos hat—one of those with a little orange, white, and blue pom pom on top because of course it was. Before she could think about it too much Astrid reached forward and plucked the hat off of Darby's head. Some of her hair stuck to it like a staticky balloon.

"I wouldn't have pegged you as a football fan." Astrid raised an eyebrow. In fact, if asked, she would have assumed Darby was a fan of just about everything *except* football. Too much yelling and hitting.

"About that, did you know the Super Bowl is Sunday?"

"I did. It's a big day for the bar but Sully let me take it off so I can watch the game."

"Perfect, so you're free on Sunday?" Darby asked.

"Well, not *free* free. I'm watching the Broncos play and hopefully win."

"I'm having a Super Bowl party."

Astrid narrowed her eyes. "Why?"

"Because it's fun to support the local team. And I had a lot of great snack ideas that were going to waste. My next-door neighbor is always cutting recipes out of Good Housekeeping and leaving them in my mailbox." Darby delivered this information as if it explained absolutely everything. She was throwing a party so her hand-me-down Good Housekeeping recipes didn't go to waste. Logical.

"Well, I guess that explains you wearing the ugliest hat I've ever seen."

Darby snatched the hat back and pulled it over Astrid's head. She put a finger to her chin as she seemed to deeply consider the scene in front of her. "Nah, I think it's pretty cute."

"Oh yeah?" Astrid took a step toward Darby. Close enough that she could smell her strawberry lip gloss. Her urge to taste it was immediate, like smelling coffee early in the morning. Astrid knew that her day would not be complete without it. She brought her hand up to Darby's cheek. Astrid could do this. She could take the risk. So what if it wasn't forever, they could have fun. If Darby was anything, it was fun.

Darby's green eyes stared into hers and something flashed in them as if she had made the decision for both of them. Darby drew nearer to her, closing the last bit of distance between them. Astrid tangled her hands in Darby's hair, twining curls around her fingers. Darby pulled the beanie from Astrid's head and tossed it aside.

Astrid had expected something fervent and rushed. But Darby's kiss was slow. Like there was nowhere else she needed to be. Like she had all the time in the world, and if given the chance she'd spend it with Astrid. And Astrid... melted.

At some point, the cat fled with an indignant mewl; Astrid threaded her arm beneath Darby's coat around her waist and pulled her closer. The press of Darby's body against hers was all warm comfort. She wanted more. Astrid ran her tongue along Darby's lower lip and Darby welcomed her in.

The slowness was quickly forgotten. Astrid found herself pressed against the wall of her entryway, Darby's hand toying with the hem of her henley.

She let the hallway hold her up. Every wall she had built was ice and Darby was the summer sun. As she tightened her grip on Darby's waist, Astrid's mind flashed to an image of an Antarctic ice shelf crashing into the sea. Except, you know, hopeful.

Another knock on the door slingshotted Astrid's racing heart to her throat.

Darby pulled back with a gleeful laugh. "Well, I've been waiting a while to do *that*."

"Me—I—Are you expecting someone?" *Very smooth,*

Astrid.

Darby gave her a faraway look like she was waking up from a dream. The way she was looking at Astrid easily made her feel three inches taller. "Hmm?"

"There's someone else at the door and I don't really get many visitors."

"Oh right!" Darby's eyes went wide. "James is going to build you a bookshelf."

"Wait wha—" She reached to pull Darby back to her like kissing again might rewind the tape and give them a few more minutes with this particular scene but the moment was over.

"Come on in, James!"

"I've kinda got my hands full here, Darbs."

"Sorry!" Darby spun and opened the door to a mildly amused looking James holding enough lumber to build the coffin she was now hoping for.

"Sorry to interrupt whatever you two were up to. Your hair's wrecked, babe." James shot Darby a wink and Astrid a look that was more like she had something unpleasant in her eye.

The next few hours should be fun then—at least Darby was here. Meatball let out a monstrous yawn and James' face lit up.

"I didn't know you had a cat, Astrid."

"Oh I don't, not really. Meatball just hangs—"

"He sleeps here?"

"Yeah."

"And you feed him?"

"I do."

"Then you've got a cat, buddy. Lean into it. I'm sorry if this is upsetting information."

"Ok, well now that you two have cats in common, I'm going to go grab us some drinks and snacks. Any requests?"

James' face went as white as the absolutely bare walls of

Astrid's apartment. "I'm good with water, Darbara."

"Yeah, um, me too. I think I have one beer in the fridge, too." Astrid rushed from the room to take a quick inventory of the kitchen. She pulled open the fridge and did a frantic scan. Was it worse to be alone with James or to leave James and Darby alone in her apartment? Both felt unbearably vulnerable, like meeting the doctor while wearing a hospital gown.

She had some shredded carrots in the crisper drawer. Was carrot water a thing? Or were cucumbers still the only acceptable vegetable water?

"Everything okay in there?" Darby called from the living room.

"Yeah, fine. I'm just seeing what I have. I don't think you need to go to—"

"Ok, I'll be back in a bit. Text me if there's anything you want me to pick up."

Astrid slammed the fridge door shut and vaulted back into the living room just in time to see the front door close. Meatball let out a soft wail and pawed at the door once in protest.

Tell me about it, buddy.

Across the room, James squinted at a pile of wood on the floor. Weren't bookshelves supposed to come in flat-pack boxes? How did she even know what to bring?

James cleared her throat. "So, um, yeah, I'm just going to get started. Mind if we put on some music?"

"Oh, sure, I'll put some on. And thank you, for this."

"Of course. I'm happy to help and Darby asked me to."

"Right." Not that Astrid had thought James was there for her, but an idea caught in her chest like a splinter. That it would be nice to have friends who did favors because she asked them to. Friends who showed up and said I will do this simple thing that you are unable to do.

Astrid hit play on her music app and the infectious

sounds of Carly Rae Jepsen filled the small apartment. Over her pile of wood, James huffed out a laugh.

"I was just um, trying to see why Darby liked it so much," Astrid mumbled, slamming her hand down on her blue tooth speaker like it was an alarm clock at five a.m. "Is there something you're in the mood to listen to?"

"I can put something on," James told her phone to put her music on shuffle.

The boppy beat was immediately recognizable and Astrid made no effort to hold back her laugh. James flushed then shrugged.

"Darby shares a lot of playlists."

"Yeah."

JAMES WORKED STEADILY while Astrid tried to keep an eye on the project while staying completely out of her way. Meatball had no such qualms as he attempted to perch on James' shoulders and chew on her hair which was getting messier by the minute.

James alternated between rubbing her cheek against the cat and swatting at him.

"I can, um, put him outside if you want."

James looked at Astrid with alarm, her light eyes flashing. "No that's okay, he's just being friendly."

"He's biting your head while you're using a power tool."

James shrugged. "I'm used to it."

Astrid opened her mouth to ask how anyone could be used to a cat biting their head while they used a drill but thought better of it. "So how long have you and Darby been friends?"

"Since just after college. We all worked together at a restaurant. Can you come to hold this up?"

Astrid lifted the shelf, resting it on its base. So far Darby had left them alone for half a bookshelf. "This looks great.

Thank you, again. Darby was really invested in me having an actual shelf for my books and records."

James grunted as she affixed another sideboard. "You know the thing with Darby is that she just kind of decides she's going to be in your life. Sometimes it takes a little while to see that her presence is a gift. I've been loved a lot but I've never been cared for like Darby cares for me. And I think Mia would say the same."

"Yeah, no, I think she's great."

"She is. Listen, you seem nice, Astrid. So please know this is coming from a good place. But Darby isn't someone to take for granted. If you want her to leave, you need to make that clear. But if you're interested in her you should make that clear, too. Basically, communicate."

"I, um—" Astrid tried to form a reply. Her head was still spinning from the way Darby kissed her earlier. Not tentative. And it was definitely nice, but she wasn't *nice* about it. And Astrid was curious what else she wouldn't be nice about. She wanted more of Darby, but she wasn't even sure if she'd still be in Colorado by spring.

"And I know it's easy to forget she needs stuff because she's so good at being there for everyone but she needs to be taken care of, too; even when you don't think she needs it. One time we all got the flu and she tried to bring me *and Mia* homemade soup. When she got to my place I just bear-hugged her and pulled her inside and that's how I watched every episode of Gilmore Girls. Poor Mia had to watch over FaceTime." James cursed beneath her breath as a screw slipped and tumbled onto the floor, never to be seen again.

"Is that what you're doing here?" Astrid leaned to one side of the shelf and caught James' eye. "Showing up and caring for her?

James nodded. "And lucky for you there are residual benefits."

"Yeah."

"Look, Astrid. She's shining her light on you. Grow towards it."

Astrid's face grew warm, and she raked her hair back from her forehead, buying time to decide if she should say what she was thinking. Her real concern about Darby. James was Darby's friend, but she seemed... steady. She drew in a deep breath and squared her shoulders. "I worry I'm not good enough for her." It came out in almost a whisper, but the slow smile that pulled at James' mouth made it clear she'd heard.

"Honestly, you're not. None of us are. I have no idea where Darby came from. But look on the bright side, she thinks you are."

A rush of frustration hit Astrid like a sharp wind. "What is this bright side everyone keeps telling me about? It's like a 3-D movie and the glasses ran out right before I got there. For me, happiness is blurry around the edges. It's hard to make out and even harder to focus on."

James shook her head. "It's Darby, she's the bright side. Don't be hard on yourself. Just try." James cleared her throat. "Okay, ready to walk this back?"

They spent the next few minutes adjusting the bookcase against the wall. Both shooting hopeful glances toward the door when they thought the other wasn't looking.

"So, uh, yeah. I think we're good here. Did you need help putting books on it or..."

"No, I've got a feeling Darby has an organization system in mind."

James chuckled. "Oh, absolutely. You're catching on quick! I think I might head out then, I've got a few more projects for the house I wanted to knock out today. Can you tell Darby I'll call her later?"

The door flew open and their heads spun in unison.

"Good news," Darby called. "I'm back and I brought tacos!"

CHAPTER ELEVEN

WHERE'S WALRUS?

DARBY

"WHAT DO YOU MEAN YOU DON'T KNOW WHAT YOU'RE wearing?"

Through the speaker on her phone, Darby heard Mia flick on her blinker forcefully and she instinctively ducked out of the way.

"I have some time."

"When is your date with Astrid?"

"I'm picking her up in an hour."

Mia sighed. "I can be at your place in ten minutes, I just need to move a meeting."

"Oh no, I was just thinking I could show you my closet on FaceTime and you could just... pick something."

"I'll be there in ten. Just don't touch anything."

The sound of Mia hanging up hung in the air for a beat.

"Um, Darbs, to be honest, I'm not really sure why I'm on this call," James said.

"For moral support, Jagermeister. And because I didn't do my hair today and I think Mia might implode."

On James' end of the line, something clattered to the floor. "Yup, I'm on my way."

Astrid slid into the passenger's seat of Darby's VW bug and draped her leather jacket over her knee.

"Hi, you look nice." Astrid turned, bringing them face to face.

Darby's breath caught and she reached to turn the music off. She didn't want to miss a thing.

Astrid's dark eyes were bright like her smile was finally reaching them. It looked good on her. Really good. Had her car always been this small? Darby swallowed. Astrid tilted her head to one side. Oh right, she was probably waiting for a response. "Thanks—Mia dressed me from her trunk."

Astrid raised an eyebrow. "Do I even want to know?"

"It's probably best to hold on to a little mystery. You look really nice too." Darby shot her a wink.

Astrid glanced down at her black jeans and boots. "I look how I always look."

"Exactly. Now buckle up, buttercup. This city is about to charm you."

"I'm not sure it's the city that's doing the charming."

A smile broke across Darby's face. "I guess it's sort of a double threat. Okay, so I know you feel good about aquatic life, but how do you feel about facial hair?"

Astrid paused in the middle of buckling her seatbelt. "I'm… neutral, I guess. And increasingly concerned about this Denver surprise date you've planned."

Darby put on her blinker and pulled away from the curb. "Is it safe to assume you're familiar with Where's Waldo, you know the stripes guy?"

"The stripes guy?" Astrid said with a laugh. "I believe I've run across him in a few dim doctor's waiting rooms."

"Great! So, you've probably noticed that Denver has a lot of street art. It's kind of hard to miss."

"I've passed some murals."

"Excellent. Well, last year someone went around and added hidden walruses in a lot of the paintings in RiNo, the arts district. I thought we could walk around and look for them."

"That sounds awesome, actually. But I'm afraid to ask what all this has to do with facial hair?"

"Oh right! Can you grab my bag from the backseat? I made us bingo cards."

Darby came to a stop at a red light. The bass from the pickup truck next to them rumbled in her chest.

Astrid squinted at her but turned slowly anyway, her shoulder brushed against Darby's arm. And there was that catch in her breath again. Maybe Astrid could grab her inhaler too.

Darby snuck glances at Astrid as she rummaged in the backseat, her black t-shirt rode up to reveal an intricate tattoo on her side that looked a bit like a monster in a children's book. As she tried to place it, Darby noticed that it was worked around a scar, the pearlescent tissue shining beneath the scales and feathers.

"What's this from?" Darby reached out her fingertips ghosting Astrid's side.

"The tattoo?" Astrid shifted in her seat. "It's an artist I like, David Shirgley."

"No, I mean the tattoo is very hot, artistically speaking of course, but I was asking about the scar beneath it."

"Ah, I was hopping a fence as a kid and it snagged me." Astrid tugged down the edge of her shirt.

"A fence snagged you that bad?"

"Well, it had some barbed wire on the top and it was before I knew better."

"Like not to scale a barbed-wire fence?"

"No, the trick about throwing your jacket over the wire to protect you. I'd forgotten to bring lunch to school and I didn't have money to buy anything, so I sort of took something from this gas station and the owner saw me. I wasn't that smart at eleven." Astrid's words were casual, like this was one in a long line of stories.

"Did you go to the hospital?"

"No. I kept running."

Darby snapped her eyes back to the road as Astrid heaved her purse into the front seat. Sadness caught sharply in her chest at the thought of Astrid running. At the thought of Astrid running still, her near-empty apartment and new city every year, Darby swallowed down the emotion, wrapping it up safely for another time. Today was about making Astrid feel happy and wanted in the here and now.

She reached over and searched until she felt the cards, handing one to Astrid. Astrid, whose eyes were wide.

"Wow, sorry, I did not think about the fact that you were holding my purse in your lap as I was feeling for those cards. Off to a great start. Anyway, moving on, the other part is that the walruses—walri?"

"Walruses." Astrid nodded seriously.

"The walruses have different facial hair and you can find them all. So if you look at your card I just did little sketches. I was thinking whoever gets a bingo first can pick the next activity."

"Ok, so when I win, by finding all of these…"

"Get ready for a competition because I am a master at finding things."

"Yeah, that adds up." Astrid nodded as she squinted against the bright winter sun.

"May I?" Darby paused before reaching for her purse and pulling it onto the console. She fished out her favorite sunnies and handed them to Astrid.

Astrid held up the pink heart-shaped sunglasses and examined them. And then looked down at her all-black ensemble. "You really are heart eyes personified."

"They'll look cute, I promise." Darby pushed down a

sudden urge to throw on her hazards and kiss away her skepticism.

Astrid slipped on the sunglasses and grinned at Darby. "These make everything so pink and happy. Do you wear these a lot?"

"As much as I can get away with." Darby shrugged. "I like to surround myself with things that make me happy."

"I get that. But life isn't about just being happy."

Darby could see the smile Astrid was fighting, her grin crooked and endearing. It was scientifically impossible to be sad while wearing pink heart sunglasses. She'd done studies.

"Of course it's not. Life is challenging and sometimes terrible and deeply unfair. I just don't focus on that stuff."

"But how? Do you just ignore the things you don't like?"

"No. I don't ignore things. I deal with them. I give each crisis the attention it needs, but not a single second more." She glanced at Astrid before continuing. Her all-black ensemble interrupted only by the sunset pink hearts over her eyes, like a cartoon cat in love. "I spent years trying to be perfect. The perfect daughter with the perfect grades. I was constantly worried about making a mistake and then one day I made a mistake and the world didn't end."

"What happened?"

"I got a B in calculus."

"You know that's not really a mistake, right?"

"In my house, it was an atrocity. My parents got me a tutor."

"And then you aced the AP exam?"

"Not even close. She became my first girlfriend, and I ended the term with a C+ and sun visor covered in mixed CDs. But I was happy, and I learned a lot. Not about math maybe, but that I could be happy even when things aren't perfect. That I could choose happiness."

"Hmm, do you offer tutoring on that philosophy?"

"Today is lesson one."

"Annnnnd mutton chops makes five in a row for me!" Astrid marked her bingo card with a flourish.

They were standing outside a brick building, a mural filled with swirls of magenta and teal stretched its expanse. There in the top left corner flanked by sugar skulls was a walrus the size of Meatball sporting the mutton chops of Wolverine. Dang.

"Wait, all I needed was the handlebar mustache." Darby crossed her arms over her chest and narrowed her eyes. "You know, you found those walri suspiciously fast."

"Walruses." Astrid grinned at Darby with her off-kilter smile. The pink heart sunglasses over her eyes caught the last bits of the sun as it made its evening descent. "Winner winner dumpling dinner!" Astrid blew a big bubble with her pink gum.

"Dumpling dinner?" Darby laughed. She liked this side of Astrid. They'd spent the afternoon wandering the streets and poring over the art that covered so many buildings, searching for the mustachioed marine mammals. It felt like building a puzzle, something they were working on together rather than a competition.

"Yeah, I was reading about this place where you can make your own dumplings, each meal is like a mini cooking class."

"Astrid, did you do research for this… hang out?" Darby's heart skipped. Was Astrid *yes and*-ing her? She was used to being humored, but Astrid seemed gleeful and sincere.

"Maybe a little. Or a lot. After you said your idea didn't involve food, not even ice cream."

"To be fair, I did bring trail mix for us. And bubble gum."

"But you ate all the chocolate out of it."

"Right, that's the best part."

"I agree. And for the record, I was thinking of this as more of a date." Astrid's fingers closed around Darby's mittened hand. "Come on, let's walk over before we freeze."

A gust of wind whipped Astrid's hair into her face, and Darby reached forward to push it back. "That reminds me, I have something for you." Darby pulled a pair of black mittens out of her bag and handed them to Astrid. "I finished them last night."

Astrid slipped the mittens on and immediately checked the palms.

"Are they okay?" She nervously bit her lip, searching Astrid's face for any hint of what she might think of the mittens. She'd stayed up almost half the night for the past few days to make sure she'd get them done, and giving them to Astrid now made her feel a bit like she was offering more than just mittens. Like she was quite literally wearing her heart on her palm. She swallowed, feeling nervous and vulnerable in a way she hadn't entirely considered.

"Yeah, I was worried you didn't put heart palm patches on them."

"Of course I did, I just made those black too. That way you can be adorable *and* incognito."

"They're perfect." Astrid took Darby's hand again and they made their way to the dumpling house mitten in mitten.

CHAPTER TWELVE

CHAPTER 12 ASTRID

ASTRID

THEY GOT BACK TO ASTRID'S PLACE WITH A CARDBOARD container full of dumplings and hands they couldn't keep to themselves.

It was absurd to find someone taking off their mittens sexy, right? But as Darby tossed hers to the floor of the entryway and locked eyes on Astrid, something shifted, like the fire between them that had been smoldering all day was suddenly throwing up sparks.

All through dinner, Astrid had been transfixed as she watched Darby fill and seal the dumplings. Her fingers with their bright teal polish pinching the dough into perfect little morsels. She'd watched Darby's mouth as she stole bites of the fillings. The way she'd groaned and licked her lips afterward drew every ounce of Astrid's attention. She never imagined two hours of making dumplings could be a kind of torture. And yet.

She'd had exactly one seltzer water and she felt absolutely drunk as they crashed into each other just inside the door to her apartment. Astrid was beginning to think of this as the

Darby effect. A floaty feeling where colors were more vibrant and smells more delicious.

"So should we put these in the kitchen?" Darby's breath was heavy against Astrid's lips and she wanted to drink it in. She glanced down to see Darby was holding the takeout container slightly aloft with an amused smile pulling at the corner of her mouth. "Astrid? What do you think?"

What had Astrid missed? Had she been staring? She definitely had. But had she been *obviously staring*? "Um, sure."

"I had fun with you tonight." Darby took a step back.

Astrid felt herself leaning forward to close the distance. "Is the night over?"

"You tell me."

Her thumb ran over the warm skin of Darby's hip as she pulled her forward. "Well, I think Meatball would like to spend some time with you."

"And what about you?"

Astrid nodded, the words caught in her throat. She wanted anything but for Darby to leave. They could sit and do crosswords for all she cared as long as she could listen to Darby laugh at her own jokes and smile at her like she was something to behold. Being with Darby felt like being on a ride she didn't want to end. But she couldn't commit to anything beyond tonight.

"Can you give me a little more than that?"

Darby was looking at her expectantly, her eyes slightly narrowed. Apparently, Astrid's nod did not convey her level of enthusiasm and turmoil. "I want you to stay, but I think maybe we should talk."

"Great, so let's talk." Darby shrugged off her coat and glanced around the space. "You only have one chair."

"Let's go to my bed."

Darby's laugh bubbled up just before she clamped a hand over her mouth.

"Ok, I just realized how suggestive that sounded. But I mean as a place to sit. And talk."

"Talking in bed, got it. Like a slumber party! Did you ever go to those and stay up all night?"

"Sure, but there was a lot less kissing at those."

"Oh? That's too bad." Darby winked and then stepped out of Astrid's embrace.

Astrid's mouth went dry as she followed the sway of Darby's hips until she disappeared into the doorway of her room. And then she followed her lead.

Darby sat cross-legged on the bed smiling at Astrid. Her eyes flickered in the low light of the lamp she'd left on earlier.

Astrid could do this. She could make a move and have something casual with Darby and not get crushed by it. Astrid settled onto the bed and shifted closer to Darby.

"Sorry, it's a little warm in here, do you mind if I take this sweater off? Who knew cashmere was so warm? Well, besides Mia."

"No, um, go for it." The window in which her mind would still be functional for an actual conversation was rapidly shrinking. Tension radiated out all the way to Astrid's fingertips. If she tried to touch Darby would they be unsteady? Would they spark?

Darby peeled the tight cranberry-colored sweater over her head to reveal a grey t-shirt sporting a pitbull wearing nerdy pink glasses.

Astrid felt some of the anxiety that had been winding in her chest ease as she let out a slight laugh. "Nice shirt."

"Thanks, I made it in a screen printing class!"

"It's very you."

Darby nodded. "Look Astrid, I'm more interested in what happens next."

"Next?"

"Yeah. At the end of a date." Darby bounced a few times on the bed, seemingly to underscore her point.

Astrid's heart was in her throat. She wanted what came next. Or what often came next. But how could she ask someone she never wanted to leave her side to just be casual?

"I know you don't do commitment to... anything." Darby gestured grandly to the mostly empty space of the room, a single half-empty wardrobe along one wall and a stack of books next to her bed. "And that's okay. I'm not going to pressure you into something you're not willing to give. I just wanted to say that for me, there doesn't have to be strings. I like spending time with you. And I'm really attracted to you. This can be a one-time thing or a two-time thing and we can still be friends." Darby rushed the words into the space between them and then sunk her teeth into her lower lip.

Astrid wanted the sting of that bite on her skin. She didn't have doubts about that. But she always let people down and Darby was just too good. Her conversation with James flashed into her mind. Communicate. Astrid took a deep breath. "I'm worried about messing this up. I don't want to get weird and end up never seeing you again."

"I promise you won't mess anything up. I'd never push you to do anything you didn't absolutely, enthusiastically want to do. We can watch a movie or do a photoshoot of Meatball tonight instead, I don't care. Well, I mean I *do* care, but I also don't, if that makes sense."

Astrid nodded, holding back a smile. "Well, I don't feel very enthusiastic about either of those options."

"Ok, then you suggest something."

Astrid leaned forward, closing the space between them until their noses touched. "May I?"

Darby's nod brought their mouths even closer and a slight tilt of Astrid's chin was all it took to reignite the soft rush of their kiss from the entryway.

Darby let out a breathy noise as Astrid nipped at her

lower lip. The sweetness of Darby's mouth flooded her senses. Astrid needed more. More contact. More of Darby. More everything.

She laced her fingers through Darby's belt loops and urged her forward. Darby kneeled, hovering over Astrid's lap. Darby pulled away slightly, each time Astrid rose up to search for her mouth. The hand Darby placed on her shoulder as she lowered herself down onto Astrid's lap was firm. Astrid could feel the heat of Darby through her jeans. She was desperate for more friction but something in the serious way Darby was looking at her made Astrid hold herself still. Astrid had the distinct feeling she was in no way ready for what was about to happen next and she couldn't wait.

Darby ran a finger under Astrid's chin, and she followed her lead until their eyes locked. A shiver ran down Astrid's spine and she stilled her fingers which had been exploring the silky skin of Darby's lower back.

"You're sure?"

Astrid was surprised to hear her own reply come out steady and strong. "I'm sure."

The pressure that had been building in Astrid's chest eased as Darby's mouth crashed back into hers, hot and insistent. It was delicious, like the first inhale after she removed her binder for the day.

Darby raked a hand through her messy brown hair, flipping it back from her face. She dropped her head back as Astrid ran careful fingers along her ribs up to the satin of Darby's bra. Astrid might not wear women's lingerie but she knew how to appreciate it. She traced a thumb over the sheer lace covering Darby's nipple.

Darby responded to her touch, her nipple pressing against the fabric, and it was the hottest fucking thing Astrid could imagine. She ran her lips along Darby's neck. One hand continued to tease Darby's nipple while the other skimmed the top of her jeans until she pinched the button.

"Is this okay?" Astrid whispered, her lips ghosting across the smooth skin of Darby's neck as she spoke.

"Mmmhmm."

Astrid flicked open the button and trailed her thumb over Darby's newly exposed skin until she felt the lace of Darby's underwear. A groan escaped Astrid.

Beneath her mouth goosebumps rose on Darby's skin. Astrid ran her tongue over them trying to taste Darby's anticipation. She tried to commit it to memory in case tonight was all they had.

Darby tilted her hips, increasing their contact and Astrid felt it like a lightning bolt low in her stomach. She was done for.

She rocked forward, hands gripping Darby's ass as she tipped her back until Darby was laid out on the mattress. Astrid settled on top of her. Everywhere their bodies touched felt like sparklers, desire nipping at Astrid's skin. Darby's hands threaded into the back pockets of her jeans and squeezed. "You know, I was noticing earlier that you have a really great butt."

"You just noticed that today?" Astrid said as she ran her hands beneath Darby's shoulders. Her hands traveled south until her fingers edged between Darby's jeans and what Astrid increasingly anticipated was the bottom half of a matching lingerie set. *Jesus.*

"I wouldn't say just."

Astrid was surprised by her own laugh as Darby's hands squeezed again. Sex had always been such a serious thing but even here, on top of her, there was a lightness to being with Darby.

"You're so sexy when you laugh."

"Laughing always makes me feel self-conscious of my crooked smile," Astrid said quietly.

"I think it's perfect. I could watch you smile all day. Although, I am pretty interested in watching you come."

Now that Darby has said the word, Astrid could think of nothing else except feeling Darby come beneath her, their bodies gliding together. She raised herself on her forearms and pulled at the bottom of Darby's shirt, sitting back until there was enough space between them to slide it off. She ran her eyes over Darby's chest, taking in the purple satin and black lace her fingers had been reading like Braille.

Astrid shifted down the bed, running her hands along Darby's thighs from her knees to her hips, easing her legs open until there was space for her between them.

"Stay. Just. Like. That." Astrid eased off the bed and stood.

She leaned forward and lowered the zipper of Darby's pants. Running her hands underneath them until she could see the black lace band and a glimpse of purple. She groaned as she grabbed the denim and pulled, Darby lifted her hips to assist but kept her legs in place. Astrid was in so much trouble.

Astrid threw the jeans behind her and the button hit the wall with a satisfying click. She stripped off her own black shirt and threw that too and then removed her own jeans for good measure. As far as she was concerned there would be no more need for clothes. Possibly ever.

"Can these come off too or..." Darby's thumbs were beneath the waistband of her underwear.

"I just want another minute to look at you like this." Astrid ran her fingers over the lace band and down until she could feel Darby's heat. She dipped her fingers beneath the fabric.

Darby gasped and pressed against her hand. Nothing was more of a turn-on than Darby being this ready for her. Astrid withdrew her hand and brought a finger to her mouth. Darby's eyes didn't leave Astrid's as she tasted her but her own flickered shut for a moment.

And then Darby was kneeling and kissing her hungrily.

She pulled Astrid forward and Astrid let go. She let herself fall and trusted Darby to catch her.

She reached between them and pushed Darby's underwear down. Darby kicked her legs, making short work of ridding herself of the barrier between them.

Darby was slick against her fingers and Astrid did her best to explore slowly. She focused on each hitch in Darby's breath, she slowed her lips on Darby's neck to feel her pulse stutter.

"Astrid." Darby's head fell back on the mattress and she blew out a breath. "I feel like you're worshipping me, which is very nice, truly, but also I want—"

Darby moaned as Astrid circled her clit. "That?"

"And—"

Astrid dipped a finger into Darby and her hips rose, drawing Astrid in further.

"Yes, that. More of that, please."

Astrid tilted her head to the side and did nothing to hold back her prideful grin. "Has anyone ever told you you're very polite?"

"Astrid."

She entered Darby with two fingers backed by the press of her own hips.

"Thank you," Darby gasped.

Astrid chuckled then lowered her mouth to Darby's collarbone. She bit down lightly and was rewarded with Darby's hips rising off of the bed. Good to know.

She withdrew slightly and added another finger as Darby pulled at Astrid's underwear and bra.

"I wish you weren't wearing so much."

"If it helps, I probably won't be later."

She kissed her way down Darby's chest, running her tongue over one nipple and then the other until Darby's back arched. She moved her hand with Darby's hips, matching her pace and adjusting until the breathy sounds that filled the room turned into moans and then just her name, repeated over and over like a prayer.

Astrid pulled back to take in Darby's green eyes and the way she bit her lower lip like she wanted it to last.

Astrid leaned down and trailed her mouth along Darby's ear. "Come for me. Don't worry, there will be more later."

ASTRID BLINKED INTO THE DARKNESS. Darby was wrapped around her, her breasts pressing into Astrid's back. She shifted closer and then heard the sound again. A soft scratching on the front door followed by a pitiful mewl he usually reserved for dinner time.

She rolled into a seated position and leaned forward, patting the floor until she felt soft fabric. She pulled on the t-shirt and went to let in the diva stray cat that she was beginning to suspect was actually hers.

Alone in the dark stillness of her apartment, she could still hear the echo of Darby's delighted laughter when Astrid came. The thought of tasting herself again on Darby's lips sent a current of desire through her. Women never stayed over and yet Darby was asleep in her bed and all Astrid wanted was more. She needed to go back to sleep before she made too much of that.

When she woke again sunlight was streaming through the window. Darby was spooning her and Meatball was spooning Darby. *Perfect.* As Astrid shifted an arm wound under her shirt until all she could feel was the warm press of Darby's palm over her heart.

Darby blinked her eyes open. "Good morning. I hope it's okay that I stayed."

"Yeah, why wouldn't it be?"

"No reason, just making sure. My shirt looks good on you."

Astrid looked down to where Darby's hand was now moving beneath the fabric, palming her breast. "I didn't realize I had put on your shirt. I had to get up to let Meatball in.

"You should keep it. It will be the brightest thing you own."

"It's gray."

"Exactly. Any idea what time it is? I need to get home early to set up for the football party."

"You've gotta stop calling it a football party. It's the Super Bowl. And it is a true miracle the Broncos made it. I'm talking divine intervention in the playoffs."

"Okay fine. I need to set up for my super football party."

"I think it's nine almost."

"Is there a clock in here?"

"Nope. I'm just judging by the sun."

"You know we don't have to do that anymore, right?"

"What?"

"Look at the sun and guess."

"Very funny. I'll go find my phone." Astrid threw off the covers and walked to the wardrobe. She pulled on her black sweatpants. "It's freezing in here."

Darby patted the bed beside her. "Now that you've left me I do feel a chill."

"Well, help yourself to some clothes. I'm going to put on coffee."

"Perfect, can you make mine half cream and half sugar?"

"Which part is the coffee?"

"Just like an inch in the bottom of the mug."

Astrid shook her head and chuckled as she left the room. No wonder Darby was always so happy. She was on a permanent sugar high.

• • •

Astrid balanced two white mugs and her phone as she entered the room to find Darby standing in just her underwear staring into her wardrobe. The sight of her wearing only underwear made Astrid's pulse leap and images from the night before flash right back into her mind. She stifled an excited smile, trying to appear a little less like she was willing to throw the coffee across the room for a few more moments in bed with Darby.

Darby's back was to Astrid so she cleared her throat. "Everything okay?"

"Yeah, just taking this in."

"Taking what in? I hardly have anything."

"Exactly." Darby took her mug from Astrid. "This mug is missing its design. Wait, so is yours."

"Yeah, they're just plain."

"I wasn't aware they made mugs like that. Would you consider yourself a minimalist?"

"Not really, minimalism is a lifestyle. This is just a strategy."

"You only have like five shirts and they're all black."

"I think I have eight. I like when everything matches everything else. It simplifies getting dressed."

"Oh, so it's sort of like a capsule wardrobe! I saw an interesting series on Instagram about those last fall."

"Darby, I have no idea what a capsule wardrobe is."

"It's a collection of clothes that are curated and have kind of a classic look so they all work together."

"Oh. This isn't like that. I just like to get dressed easily and when something wears out or gets lost in a move it's easy to replace."

"I'm just saying that sounds a lot like a minimalist, capsule wardrobe lifestyle."

"Can you please just put something on so we can eat dumplings for breakfast?"

"Funny that you've reversed your stance regarding me and clothes since last night." Darby winked at Astrid. "You might not know this, but you don't actually have to get dressed to eat breakfast. Well, unless you're at a restaurant, then I think it's strongly encouraged."

CHAPTER THIRTEEN

I JUST HOPE BOTH TEAMS HAVE FUN

DARBY

"Darbs, what is this exactly?" Mia lifted a jam jar of Nickelodeon-orange liquid.

"It's strawberry lemonade."

Mia raised an eyebrow skeptically. "Has it become radioactive?"

"No, it's become festive!" Darby pointed to the Broncos hat on her head, the orange, white, and blue pom pom topping it bobbing with her nod.

"Okay, that was a... choice, I guess." Mia chuckled and took a sip. "If this stains my mouth I'm suing you for defamation."

Darby grinned. "I made it orange to keep your pink lemonade secret," she stage whispered to James.

"Uh-huh." James' eyes were glued to Zee where she stood across the room with her sister El.

"James!" Darby said flabbergasted. "You're staring with your mouth open."

James shook her head, glancing away from Zee's retreating form.

Delight flared in Darby's chest. James Jagermeister

Dayhoff checking out a woman's ass in broad daylight. It must be love.

She turned her attention back to Mia who was picking at some of the latkes Darby had made earlier. "Mimi, why aren't you wearing your jersey?"

"I put it in my purse for safekeeping. I didn't want to stain it by accident."

"Don't worry about that, I can always make you another one."

"Yeah, Mia," James interjected. "We're both wearing *our* jerseys."

"Fine Jagerbomb." Mia retrieved the orange and white jersey from her bag and pulled it over her tan sweater. "Are you two happy now?" Readjusting her raven hair so it fell just right over her shoulders, muttering something about orange clashing with her umber complexion.

"I was happy before. But I'd be happier if you ate more snacks and watched the puppy bowl with me."

"I'll be right there, Darbs. I think Astrid just got here."

"Hey, you made it!" Darby pulled Astrid into a hug and resisted the urge to kiss her in a decidedly not casual way. "I hope it's okay that I brought a friend."

"Okay? It's incredible! How did I not know that you knew Lauryn?"

"I feel like I should be surprised that you know Lauryn but honestly last night you almost made friends with a pigeon."

Astrid smiled in a way that made Darby's heart squeeze. She loved that Astrid had such a connection with stray animals. Wait, be casual, Darby. She greatly liked that about her. *She like* liked it.

"Pigeons are obsessed with me for some reason. They're actually very smart."

"Love the confidence, Ash. Thanks for having me, Darby." Lauryn leaned in and kissed her cheek, the puff of her hair, which sat messily atop her head tickled Darby's cheek.

"I'm so glad you're here and Mia will be too! Please compliment her jersey!"

"On it." Lauryn winked and pulled off her coat as she headed toward the kitchen.

ASTRID'S EYES went wide as she surveyed her surroundings. "Did you do all of this in the five hours since you left my place? All I did was take a shower."

"Well, that's important, too." Darby took half a step closer to Astrid, balling her hands into fists so she didn't reach for her. Casual was probably not holding hands in front of her friends. "But this is nothing. Come see the snacks."

"I like your jersey."

Darby glanced down, she'd spent a week designing and making the "I just hope both teams have fun" jerseys. "Oh, really? My friends were kind of acting like they're torture but I thought they'd be fun."

"No, they're perfect, very you. And your face paint is great too."

The orange face paint had been a game-time decision, but Darby was pleased with the evenness of the lines. "I have another one if you want it? I know you don't like a lot of stuff but—"

Astrid's hand was warm on Darby's wrist, her thumb drawing circles over her pulse point. "I'd love one. And you know I have space in my wardrobe for it."

"Ok, I'll go get it! Do you want to go check out the snacks? I think there's like five tons of food in there and I made a chip tasting station with little cups of like twenty different kinds."

"Sure, but before I let you go, you'll be right back?" Astrid squeezed her wrist gently.

Darby's heart was a balloon that wanted to float to the ceiling, like Astrid's hand on hers was anchoring her to the room. "Yeah, I won't leave you alone, even though everyone here is very nice. But if you don't want to talk just take a big bite of something and by the time you finish, I'll be back."

"I think that's the kindest way to avoid a conversation I've ever heard."

Darby returned gripping the jersey. It had taken her a bit longer than expected to stencil Meatball Sub on the back, but the end product was worth it.

Astrid, for her part, was deep in conversation with James and Mia.

"Hey, here you go." Darby slid into place between Astrid and Mia. This was nice.

"Oh no, she got you too?" James laughed.

"Nah, I begged for one. These are incredible. Wait, Darby, does it say Meatball Sub on the back because I'm submissive to Meatball?"

Mia made a sputtering sound as she coughed up some of her drink. And Darby reached over and patted her back. Maybe staining her clothes really was a risk.

She turned back to Astrid. "We should all be submissive to cats. The ancient Egyptians had that part right."

"Totally. Well, I love it." Astrid took a sip of her orange pink lemonade and turned toward James. "So which one of you is really into football?"

"Don't look at me. I know I'm on the butch side of the spectrum but my interest ends at power tools."

"Oh, well I already know Darby's not a big fan. Mia?"

"I'm here for the snacks."

"Here, here," Darby said, raising her glass.

•   •   •

SHE HAD FAILED to consider the length of a football game. The quarters were a reasonable fifteen minutes but somehow that had absolutely no real relation to actual time. At least half time was coming up and they could take a break from the television. It was too bad James and Zee had to leave so early, but at least James had kept her jersey on for the whole time.

She stood up and Astrid grabbed her hand. "Where are you going?"

"I need to grab something from my room and then I'm going to refresh the snacks before the halftime break."

"I'll come with you."

"You don't have to do that, I know you want to watch the game. If there's something you want I can grab it for you while I'm up."

"I don't mind missing some of the game." Astrid stood and followed Darby out of the living room and down the hall.

It didn't escape Darby that she never let go of her hand. But she knew where Astrid stood. It was kind of silly that sex could be casual but not holding hands, right? Okay then, casual hand-holding.

"Your room is so cute, you have so much stuff in it but it doesn't feel overwhelming."

"Yeah, I have a calm color scheme in here. The white bed makes things feel more open. Otherwise, keeping surfaces clear goes a long way when you have a lot of furniture in a space."

"Huh, I've never associated having a lot of stuff with a space being calm."

"With good design most things are possible. I could always help you decorate your place if you want."

Astrid seemed hesitant. "Yeah, maybe."

"I meant to ask, did you get your heat working right this morning?"

"Something's wrong with the thermostat, just like my last place. I'm beginning to think it's a Denver renters curse. I have a repair person coming tomorrow between eight and five."

"So just some time during daylight hours then?"

"Pretty much."

"Well, you're welcome to stay here tonight, if you want. You know, so you don't freeze. Meatball can come over too."

"I'll call and let him know."

"Don't make fun, I'm just thinking of him." Darby gave Astrid an indignant stare.

"I know you are. It's sweet."

Astrid had a serious look on her face as she closed the space between them.

"He's a nice cat and I—"

Astrid's mouth was on hers before she could finish her worry about the cat's wellbeing. This kiss was different from last night, less gentle and more insistent. Astrid bit Darby's lower lip and she moaned.

When Astrid pulled back and rested her forehead against Darby's, her face was flushed and her breath short. Darby flashed back to the way Astrid had said her name between moans last night. Same energy. "I was finding it very hard to be around you and not do that."

"Me too. I was trying to play it cool, but there is something that's been on my mind."

Astrid stiffened slightly. "What's that?"

"How about I close the door and you do me a favor and take off your pants?"

Astrid's eyes flashed as she shimmied out of her pants in what Darby felt confident was a record speed.

"Perfect. Those too." Darby nodded to Astrid's black briefs. She absolutely had to find a way to infiltrate her wardrobe with some other colors.

Astrid pulled off her jersey and black t-shirt then slid down her briefs. "Ok, your turn."

"Actually, if you don't mind, I kind of like it like this."

Astrid raised an eyebrow but nodded. "Jane Darby, are you making a power move?

"I think you're about to find out."

"Is there somewhere you want me?"

"Seated on the edge of the bed. Please," she added hastily.

"You're so polite."

"Not for long." Seeing Astrid naked before her sent a rush of heat to Darby's core. She found keeping her clothes on allowed her to focus more fully, like putting her phone on airplane mode. No interruptions or distractions.

Astrid settled on the bed and Darby urged her knees apart before kneeling between them. "Is this okay?"

"This is… incredible."

Darby hummed as she placed Astrid's knees over her shoulders and kissed up the inside of her thigh. She dipped down to taste Astrid before trailing her tongue back up to focus on Astrid's clit, experimenting with a slightly different rhythm than last night.

Astrid's hands fisted into her hair and Darby moaned against her clit. She tugged again as though experimenting.

"Darby, I'm not going to make it long if you keep doing that."

Darby lifted her head and met Astrid's dark stare. "Me neither."

Astrid's fist tightened in Darby's hair, tugging it a bit harder than before. Darby's own excitement ticked up and the pressure built between her thighs. It grew in intensity until Astrid's soft whimpers turned into moans, then into a chant of Darby's name. Astrid's thighs tightened as she drew close to orgasm, blocking out the noise of the party, blocking out everything except the way Astrid felt against her tongue, the taste of her flooding Darby's senses. Beneath the knees of her jeans, the carpet was a steady reminder of the scene, rooting her in place, ratcheting up her own desire for Astrid.

Astrid collapsed back on the bed and the grip of her legs

loosened. Darby leaned back, unzipping her jeans. Her own wetness coating her fingers. Astrid propped herself up on her elbows. "What are you doing? Do you want help?"

"No, I just want to look at you while you come back down."

THEY STUMBLED their way to the kitchen to grab drinks, their shoulders knocking together playfully. "So you like it with a house full of people? I never would have guessed."

Darby shrugged and winked. "I like a lot of things."

Astrid's cheeks flushed. "Well, I look forward to that."

"Why don't you go back to the living room and I'll grab stuff for us?"

"Oh yeah, less conspicuous that way."

Darby washed her hands and grabbed two waters. She wanted to give Astrid time to get settled so she spent a long time arranging a plate of pizza rolls into the shape of a cat before making her way to the living room.

She entered to see the Broncos down in the fourth quarter, which did not seem good, necessarily. But the guy in a baby blue top and silver hot pants dancing in the end zone seemed to be having a good time at least.

Mia looked up from her seat next to Lauryn. Their fingers had *definitely* been brushing. Interesting. They were a week from Valentine's Day and love was definitely in the air. Or maybe that's what was in the lemonade.

"Are you okay, babe?" Mia patted the armrest next to her for Darby to take a seat.

"Yeah, why?"

Mia motioned her closer and whispered in her ear, "Because your face paint is wrecked and I'm willing to bet there's quite a bit of it on Astrid."

"I was warm in here, so I splashed some water on my face.

Too bad they don't make waterproof face paint like they do eyeliner I guess." Darby shrugged.

"And was that before or after you took Astrid to your bedroom for a full quarter."

"I don't see how that's relevant. Can I get you anything? Are you two thirsty?"

"Were fine." Mia placed a hand on Darby's knee to hold her in place. "I want to hear *everything* later. You didn't even call this morning to tell me about your date yesterday."

"I know. I'm so sorry. I stayed over Astrid's and then got kind of a late start so I had to rush to get everything done."

"Mmhmm. A likely story."

Lauryn leaned across Mia. "What are we talking about?"

"Mia's grilling me about my sex life like she doesn't realize I've benevolently decided not to grill her about *hers*. Or should I say yours?"

Lauryn widened her eyes at Mia. "Yup, you're on your own with this one. I'm going to watch grown men grab each other's asses *in friendship* on live TV."

A groan went up from the room. The Lions were doing another dance routine with the ball. Pretty cute choreography.

Mia dropped her head back against the couch. "Can we please shut it off now? They're not coming back from this."

"Sports are just about spending time together and having fun. It doesn't matter who wins or loses." Darby took a long drink of her water. She needed to turn the heat down before her face paint got even worse.

"Darbs, I love you. That is not even remotely true. I don't even watch sports and even I know the entire point is who wins."

"Look, that guy just threw a pass that arched like a rainbow and that other guy caught it! It's like witnessing a miracle."

"When the outcome is the opposite of what you want, it's usually considered a travesty."

Darby shrugged. "I wanted to spend the day hanging out with you all and eat a ton of pizza rolls." She held one of the little parcels of goodness in the air to emphasize her point. "So today's a win in my book."

"Oh, I bet it is." Mia gave her a sly grin and then let her hand fall back on top of Lauryn's.

A win indeed.

CHAPTER FOURTEEN

MUFFINS ARE NOT CASUAL

ASTRID

Astrid's hand groped along the floor for her ringing phone until her knuckles banged into something solid. She winced.

Right, Darby's house had places to put things and things to put in said places.

She opened one eye and grabbed her phone off of the nightstand before slipping out of bed and padding out of the room.

Behind her, Darby sighed and rolled into the warm space she'd left behind. God, that was cute.

Nope, nope, nope. *Casual. Finding ordinary things someone does cute is decidedly non-casual behavior.* And non-casual thoughts only led to one place. The intersection of heartbreak and disappointment.

"Hey Ellen, is everything okay?"

The voice on the other end of the line murmured something indistinguishable and then increased to foghorn volume. "Astrid? It's Ellen from Fairview."

Why did everyone from her Senior Center job put the

phone on speaker to hear better? She lifted the phone away from her ear with a cringe.

"Hi Ellen, I know. Why are you calling so early?"

"Early? It's almost seven! Look, can you do a shift today?"

"Today's really hard for me. I have someone coming to fix my heat so someone needs to be at my apartment."

"So ask someone else, one of the neighbors you're friends with."

Was she supposed to be making friends with her neighbors? She heard Darby starting to stir and felt a strong urge to end the call. "Um—"

"Look, Astrid, I know it's not your usual shift but Portia is sick and everyone was looking forward to movie day. It's supposed to be Casablanca."

"If you need me to walk you through how to use the DVD player, I can explain that."

"Please come in. You know what it's like to have a mob of 85-year-old women blaming you for ruining their day. You can't do that to me."

Astrid turned in time to see Darby pull a shirt over her head. Damn. "Ok, let me see what I can do and I'll call you back in a bit." She ended the call and walked back into Darby's bedroom. She was busy putting throw pillows back on the already made bed. Like last night had never happened.

"Hey, good morning." Darby smiled at her as she threw the last pillow, a red, yellow, and blue southwestern diamond pattern onto the pile of others already on the bed. "Is everything alright with your place?"

"Oh yeah, that was work. Someone called in so they want me to cover, but I have the guy coming to fix the heat."

"Is Revel even open during the day?"

"No, this is a different job. Fairview Senior Center over in Littleton."

"Oh, I didn't know that." Darby tilted her head, her messy

brown curls falling into her face like they had a mind of their own. "How many jobs do you have?"

Astrid reached forward without thought and brushed some of it back so she could see Darby's eyes and the freckles dusting her nose and cheeks. Darby pressed her cheek into Astrid's palm in response. Little alarm bells rang in the back of Astrid's mind.

"Three." Astrid shrugged. "I like to keep my options open."

"That makes a lot of sense."

"Monday's shouldn't be allowed to start out bad."

"You're right! Do you want solutions or solidarity?" Darby smiled at her.

There was a vulnerability to people first thing in the morning. Like all other aspects of their personalities were distilled until all that was left was the purest version of them. And that version of Darby was looking at her like she was about to swoop out of the sky and save her from falling.

"Aren't you going to tell me to look on the bright side?" Astrid asked.

"Is that what you want me to tell you?"

"Well, I mean, isn't that your thing?"

"Right, it's *my* thing because it works for me." Darby shrugged, a sleepy smile crossing her face. "I'm under no illusions that it's comforting for everyone."

"Oh." Astrid hadn't expected that. It was sometimes easy to conflate Darby with happiness like nothing rocked her. But she'd explained the other night that it was a choice she made.

Darby placed a hand on Astrid's waist. Her fingertips still radiated under-the-covers warmth onto Astrid's skin. "So, I'll ask again. Do you want solutions or solidarity?"

"I want my place to not be freezing, but I also don't want to ruin Esther and the knitting gang's week. I'm afraid they might knit me a truly hideous sweater as retribution."

"Ok, so both then. Also, those ladies sound incredible. Ask

them if they have any good mitten patterns—I need a new challenge. Here's my proposal: how about I go to your place while you make some old ladies happy?"

"Really? Don't you have to work?"

"Let me check with my boss." Darby held up her index finger signaling Astrid to hold on for a minute as she put her other hand to her ear and mimed listening to a headset. "Okay yup, thanks." Darby hung up her fake phone call and grinned at Astrid. "Great news. She said I can FaceTime James one hundred times and work remotely."

Astrid felt the relief wash over her. Before Darby, she couldn't remember the last time someone went out of their way to help her, but Darby had helped her move, gotten James to build her a bookshelf, and now this. And she seemed delighted to be doing it. "You're a lifesaver. Some of the residents plan their whole week around movie day and today's Casablanca."

"Well, I'd never want anyone to miss out on a good love story."

ASTRID BANGED through the front door of her apartment at quarter to six that evening. The pitch-black winter sky felt appropriate for a day where literally everything had gone wrong, including the snowbank that had just packed snow into her boot. Who needs sunlight anyway? She liked working at the senior center but something about people relying on others to care for them made her achingly sad. All she wanted to do was lay down on her bed for twelve hours.

In the foyer, she was met by the warmth of a working heater and the smell of something deliciously sweet baking— maybe from the apartment next door? It felt like walking into a home, not just some random apartment that she was staying in for now.

Astrid stopped short. Tears filled her eyes faster than she could blink them back.

"Hey, you're back! How was the movie?" Darby called from the direction of the kitchen.

Astrid turned to face the door, quickly wiping at her eyes before turning back around. Heart sunglasses didn't sound so bad about now. "It was long. Someone got glitter glue on the disc and I couldn't get it to work so I had to spend three hours reading out every other movie option only to hear why it was an inferior choice. I was like the human version of Netflix browsing. Totally demoralizing."

"Okay, well, good news on the home front at least: the heat's working, and banana muffins will be out of the oven in three minutes." Darby adjusted the messy bun on her head. A streak of flour dusted one of her cheeks.

In a split second, Astrid flashed to a lifetime of moments like this. Coming home to Darby smiling, covered in whatever project that had her attention that day. Something clenched in her chest like a roller coaster about to fall. Astrid hated roller coasters.

"You didn't have to waste your time waiting for me to get back." Astrid felt the stiffness in her posture, her muscles tensed and she hated herself for it.

Darby tilted her head to one side and narrowed her eyes at Astrid. "I wasn't wasting my time. The guy left fifteen minutes ago and I was waiting for this batch of banana muffins to finish."

Astrid froze. "Where did you even get bananas? I never have any."

"Your neighbor Emily came by earlier. I guess she heard the music I was playing while I brainstormed the new light fixture for the bedroom of the house we're working on. Carly Rae Jepsen always brings people together. For the light, I'm thinking of an ornate chandelier. Anyway, she had the bananas with her and mentioned she was going out of town.

She wanted to know if we like to bake and I love to bake, so I accepted her offer of bananas. And now, in a few minutes, there will be muffins." Darby finished with a smile and a ta-da-like motion.

"Did you explain to her that you were just here for the heat to get fixed? That we're not an *us*? I don't even know how to bake, Darby." Astrid raked a hand through her hair, pacing back and forth in the narrow entryway feeling trapped. She felt like a tiger in a cage.

This was why she never let anyone get too close. This was why she never stayed in one place for too long. Because when you stay in one place for long enough, and you start caring about the people there, they leave. Everyone always left. Astrid knew that it was better if she was the one who left first, who pushed people away so they left when she was prepared for it. She crossed her arms over her chest, steeling her body. Better to be the one to rip the bandaid than the one left surprised with an open wound, right?

"Are you asking if I told your neighbor, who you've clearly never met, that you and I are just having casual sex?" Darby laughed but there was a choked quality to it that Astrid had never heard from her before. "That information didn't seem appropriate for our two-minute conversation." Darby took a step closer to Astrid, reaching out a hand before dropping it back to her side. "Help me understand what's going wrong here."

"It's just—" Astrid drew in a shaky breath and re-crossed her arms over her chest. The leather of her jacket creased beneath her palms. She hadn't even unzipped it like it was some kind of armor against whatever this feeling in her chest was. "Muffins aren't casual Darby."

"What does that even mean?"

"Would you cook like that for your friends?"

"Last week when I was spending time with Nora Ephron I made James a lasagna."

"Nora Ephron?"

"James' cat."

"Okay." Astrid let out a rush of air. "Well, this is not that."

"Astrid, I don't know what that means."

"It means that I had a really long day and," Astrid paused, bracing herself, "I can't do this. Thanks for helping with the heat and everything else, but I think you should go. I need some time to myself." Just saying it broke something inside of her, but she had to do it. She knew it was for the best. It was always best when it was her idea, when she could see the hurt coming and grit her teeth through it.

A loud ding sounded from the kitchen and Darby flinched in a way that Astrid felt in her chest.

"Okay then, you should pull those out before they burn." Darby nodded to the kitchen. "And, for what it's worth, I don't think I should have to defend doing something nice for you because I wanted to. But you should also know it was cold in here and baking helped warm it up. Sometimes a muffin is just a muffin, Astrid."

Darby brushed past Astrid and slipped into her coat. She pulled her hat on, the pom pom shaking with the movement. "Have a good night, Astrid. Meatball's asleep on your bed. He was crying around five, so I fed him dinner."

Darby opened the door to the hall and Astrid felt hollowed out. Like in the space where her heart should be was a cold, empty apartment.

"Darby, wait."

Darby turned back. Her green eyes shining in the light. Astrid hated the tears that gathered there, like the few drops of rain before the storm started in earnest. "Yeah?"

"Don't you want to take the muffins with you?"

"No, I don't need them. I have plenty at home." She pulled the door closed behind her, leaving Astrid standing there alone in her warm apartment.

CHAPTER FIFTEEN

PARTY FOR ONE

DARBY

DARBY WAS GETTING WELL ACQUAINTED WITH THE PATTERN ON James' ceiling. The plaster had been swirled into arcs like hundreds of tiny rainbows. It was nice to think of James living at the end of a rainbow.

She'd tried all her tricks to cheer herself as she drove straight to James' house after Mia didn't answer her phone. She'd blasted Too Much by Carly Rae Jepsen seven times in a row. She'd put on her heart-shaped sunglasses and broke into the bag of gummy bears she kept in her glove compartment for emergencies. And all of that had landed her here: laying on James' couch feeling dramatic about the ceiling.

Astrid's words echoed through her head. She hadn't been casual enough. She'd been too much. At least she was in Carly's good company with that.

Darby had felt so happy in those few hours at Astrid's apartment. She hadn't even let herself snoop except when she'd tried to find a comb to brush Meatball. It was nice just to be in Astrid's place. It wasn't Darby's style maybe, but it felt like Astrid, and that was somehow better than a familiar comfort. But even more than that, it had felt good to be doing something for Astrid. Darby thought she had been taking care of Astrid in a non-invasive way. Making sure she didn't freeze in the three-degree weather tonight. Feeding the cat she somehow still didn't think was hers even though Darby had found bowls and wet food in the cupboard. In fact, that was just about all she'd found in the kitchen cupboards. She'd had to run down to the store for nutmeg and flour.

And then she'd gone and Muffin Man-ed it.

But if she could do it over, what would she change? Probably nothing. She was just being herself. And there was nothing she could change now, anyway. She'd wrecked it.

Darby grabbed one of the decorative throw pillows she'd picked out for James from behind her head. They were really holding up nicely. She picked at a loose blue thread, on the mid-century couch that she'd helped James pick and then she pulled one of the pillows over her face and yelled into it. By the time she was done, her lungs burned and her head felt floaty. Mia was right, that was pretty helpful.

She reached for her purse on the coffee table to retrieve her inhaler. The albuterol rushed to her head.

"Hey, Darbara." James was in the doorway of the living room but she made no move to enter. Her voice was so gentle, like the brush of sandpaper on wood. "Do you want to help me feed Nora? She likes it best when you do—I can never pull off that little pyramid you make with her kibble."

Darby tried to smile, but one look at the wary expression on her friend's face and tears stung her eyes. "Is she asking for me?"

A desperate meow sounded from somewhere in the house and then something that sounded a lot like a bowl full of dry food hit the floor.

"Yep." James nodded and shoved her hands into the pockets of her dark jeans.

She sighed and rolled off the couch. Nora couldn't go hungry just because Darby was having a pity party, which was arguably the least fun kind of party anyway. Except maybe that silent party James had thrown five years ago. A whole night communicating through Post-it Notes.

Darby made her way over to where James was observing her from the door. "Why are you all dressed up?"

James looked down at herself and plucked at her gray t-shirt. "I'm in a t-shirt and jeans, Darbs. How low is the bar for me and dressing?"

"You know what I mean. Any time you're not in work pants I assume there's an occasion."

"There is. Dinner with you."

"So I'm not ruining a date night?"

"Nope. No dates. You're not ruining anything."

"Are things going well with Zee? Ugh, here I am making this night all about me."

"No, Darbs, everything's good with Zee. She's, um, really great."

James' face was flushed, but Darby never read too much into that. James was always blushing like she'd been sitting too close to a fire.

Mia flew in the door on a gust of wind. She set a bag full of groceries on the floor and pulled Darby into a tight hug before slipping off her heels. Darby let her head fall onto Mia's shoulder. "Hey Darbs, I've got the night free and I brought all your favorites."

AN HOUR and two glasses of wine later, the trio sat cross-legged on the floor of James' living room. Nora was stretched out in the middle of their triangle like a game board spinner.

"I mean who doesn't like muffins?" Darby said through her bite of ice cream.

"I don't think it was about the muffins, babe." Mia smoothed her hair, her perfect center part somehow still as intact at nine p.m. as her eyeliner.

Mia was the kind of stunning that was both effortless and meticulous, a sort of witchcraft Darby aspired to as she gathered her mess of curls into a bun on top of her head.

"I think Mia's right." James nodded. "It sounds like Astrid spooked. Just give her a few days."

"I'm not sure if a few days will do it. She asked for casual, but even me doing casual was more than she wanted."

"We love you, Darbs, but let's be honest. You don't do casual. That's part of what makes you so special. I remember my first shift with you at the restaurant. You introduced yourself before I even had my coat off and by the end of the night your number was in my phone and you'd talked me into a Bachelor marathon." Mia quirked an eyebrow.

"Don't you still watch The Bachelor?" James asked.

Mia shot James a capital L look. "That wasn't really my point, James." "I know I can be a lot." Darby felt Mia's words settle like a rock in her stomach. Was even her friendship too much?

"That's not what I'm saying. You're the perfect amount, but you're a force. It's like, you know when you leave a movie theater in the middle of the day?"

James reached forward and grabbed the bottle of wine. "I'm not following this at all."

Mia narrowed her eyes at James, who suddenly became very busy peeling the label on the bottle. "As I was saying in my eloquent metaphor, after a few hours in the cool darkness the sun is both nice and it burns your eyes. Sometimes you need to step back into the shade to adjust."

"In this metaphor, Astrid is going to the movies and I'm the sun burning her?"

"Well, I think I said it a lot nicer than that. Just give her time, Darbs. And until she's ready, you've got us, Nora Ephron, and the entire series of Gilmore Girls on Netflix."

"Oh my gosh, it's back on Netflix?"

Mia nodded and pulled Darby into her side. "Things are looking up, Darbs."

CHAPTER SIXTEEN

WHEN SOMEBODY SNEEZED

ASTRID

A STRID STUFFED HALF A MUFFIN INTO HER MOUTH AND CHEWED. She needed to go to Revel and pick up her check, but instead she was wrapped in a blanket. Sometime late last night the heat had quit again, like a fire she'd forgotten to feed before falling asleep.

Meatball laid at the foot of the bed batting at Astrid's feet beneath the blanket. She wiggled her toes and he pounced. His claw snagged in the fabric and he thrashed like a fish on a line. Astrid set down the other half of the muffin, her third of the morning, and freed him.

If Darby were here she'd probably file his nails. Astrid felt a smile tug at her mouth as a vision of Darby and Meatball together at a spa flashed into her head, both of them leaned back with towels wrapped around their heads and cucumbers over their eyes.

Darby was exactly the kind of person who would know about a cat spa if one existed. Astrid's fingers itched to reach for her phone and bring up her text with Darby, but what would she say?

Sorry that my reaction to you being nice was to be a total jerk? Well, that was a start.

She looked at their last message, already committed to her memory.

Darby: I hope you like good news

Darby: not to lede you on

Darby: that was a newspaper joke. I hope you don't cry too hard while watching Casablanca and lose all your street cred. Not that I'd judge you.

The last message had been seven heart-eyed cat emoji. Twenty minutes later Astrid had walked in the door, a ticking time bomb of emotions. When Darby exploded it was probably into confetti. Or the candy that gets thrown into crowds during parades.

"How badly do you think I messed it up, buddy?"

Meatball's green eyes glowed at her in the low light of the room before he thudded onto the floor and sauntered away.

"Yeah, that's what I was afraid of."

It was the weird in-between time of day, somewhere after sunrise and before the real morning started. The sky outside was gloomy but turning on the overhead light was a commitment to this Thursday she was not yet willing to make. Maybe this was why Darby owned so many lamps. Astrid turned on her phone's flashlight and pointed it toward the ceiling. Close enough. She had approximately one to one and a half muffins before she needed to rally.

THE PERSON her landlord sent to fix the heat didn't show up until almost one. So it turned out she had time to stare at the ceiling and eat the rest of the muffins after all. Astrid watched him as he squatted in front of her old iron radiator and stared at it like it was a wild animal. And then he took out a wrench and hit it. The clang echoed through her apartment. Okay then. Enough of this good time. She was now really and truly late to meet Sully at Revel.

"So I need to head to work, would it be possible for you to lock up when you're done? You can just turn the lock on the knob and that should do it."

She received a grunt and a very generous nearly full moon in response. Excellent. She took one last look at Meatball stretched out on the kitchen counter like drying pasta and left.

The door next to hers flew open as she passed it and a woman with messy blonde hair piled on top of her head craned neck into the hallway.

"Hey, you're Astrid, right?"

Astrid's heart pounded in her throat. This woman was not a threat. *Probably.*

"Yes."

"I'm Caroline, I met Darby the other day? I gave her some bananas."

"Oh right, she told me." Astrid felt shame paint her cheeks pink.

"I just wanted to say thank you for the nice card."

"The nice card?"

"Yeah, the one you two sent with the banana muffin recipe. It makes me wish I had more ripe bananas so I could make them today."

She had sent a card. Astrid had been a jerk and Darby had still sent a thank you card for some bananas that were just going to end up in the trash. Would it be weird if Astrid asked to see the recipe? The urge to run her eyes over the little hearts Darby put at the end of her sentences was overwhelming. Great, now she was pathetic.

"That's all Darby, she's the best."

"Yeah, I could tell. Well, I hope you have a great day. Tell Darby hi for me. Also, I'm having some people over tomorrow if you both want to come. Just casual."

"Oh, um, maybe. See you." Astrid pulled her beanie out of her pocket and pulled it as low over her eyes as she could. Darby had charmed her neighbor. She could charm absolutely anyone. And for some reason, she'd picked Astrid.

SULLY WAS busy unloading crates of bottles when Astrid finally pushed in the door of Revel a little after noon.

"Finally, my knight in all black armor. I'm getting too old to lift these cases."

"Sorry, I'm late. I had a thing with my heat."

"Again?"

"Yeah, it turns out when you own an old building you actually have to take care of it."

"Huh, someone should tell your landlord that. Why don't you grab a beer and help me restock the back of the bar? I haven't even started in the backroom yet."

Astrid hesitated, glancing at Sully's own glass of water. How Sully had been sober for as long as she had and still owned a bar was a level of compartmentalization Astrid aspired to. Far be it for her to upset what might be a delicate balance. Sully might own the bar but she was almost never behind it. "I'm good."

Sully stopped unloading green bottles of Hendrix from a box and turned to face her. "It's alright, Astrid. Do you really think I'd step foot behind this bar if someone ordering a drink could rock my sobriety?"

"Ok, fine."

Astrid and Sully restocked bottles in silence, only the windchime sound of glass clinking against glass between them.

"So do you want to talk about it or should we keep pretending nothing's wrong?" Sully arched an eyebrow at

Astrid, the wrinkles around her eyes as telling as a topographical map.

"Talk about what?"

"Well, last week you were all smiles, even when the relief door person bailed. I saw you wearing mittens."

"Mittens are really practical actually. They're very warm."

"So who is she?"

"Who?"

"Please." Sully rolled her eyes. "The woman who made you the mittens and convinced you to wear them."

"It's complicated."

"Yes, your aggression with those bottles of Grey Goose have indicated as much."

"I think I blew it. She did me a favor the other day, she stayed at my place for the heat to get fixed and when I got home she was baking muffins."

"Well, that sounds dreamy."

"It was, but also—"

"Also overwhelming?"

"Yeah, how did you know?"

"Because for years I didn't think I deserved nice things. I saw every bad thing that happened to me as earned by my decisions, by the ways I'd let people down. You know I used to have to excuse myself every time I got a compliment because people being nice to me made me cry?"

"I had no idea."

"Well, that's because people can change and I chose to change. And then I absolutely worked my ass off to get it done. Simple." Sully laughed.

Sometimes talking to Sully felt like reading her own horoscope. "What if I can't? I don't want to rely on her too much and become a burden. I don't want to weigh her down."

"Someone making you happy isn't the same thing as you being reliant on them."

"But I'm happier when I'm around her. What if I get hooked on that?"

"That's not a problem. That's just a positive. Look, can you get through your day without her?"

"Yes, of course."

"Ok, but do you want to?"

Astrid paused for a long time, tilting her near-empty bottle back and forth like she was trying to find a level place inside herself. "No."

"Well, there you go. Call your girl. Well, first help me finish restocking, and *then* call your girl."

"Good call. I want to figure out what to say before I talk to Darby."

"Oh my goodness, it's Darby? She's the best. She helped Angie redecorate our living room last year. Yeah, you should fix that immediately."

"Thanks, Sul. Very helpful."

THE DULL GREY February sky loomed overhead and all Astrid could think about was the brightness of January. The way the sun had warmed her skin even on the coldest days. She continued her slushy trek home from Revel. The wind picked up, whistling down the street and she shoved her bare hands into her pockets, pulling them back as though they'd been bit when her fingers brushed against the mittens. Tears filled her eyes from the stinging wind. Probably. She pulled on the black mittens, running her thumbs over the hearts on the palms. Adorable *and* incognito.

Could things with Darby be both casual and caring? Was casual what Astrid even wanted? Or was the idea of keeping things casual a protective cloak she wrapped herself in, like another part-time job she could leave at a moment's notice—just before she lost it? All she knew was that she felt the absence of Darby like a lost mitten in a blizzard.

By the time she got to her building, a light layer of snow had sprinkled from the sky, like God was a waiter grating cheese over Denver. She stomped her boots on the doormat and climbed the stairs.

Astrid approached her apartment door with a feeling in her stomach like an elevator about to plummet. Like something was wrong before it was wrong. Her apartment door wasn't closed all the way. She toed it open and glanced around for the repairman, but the apartment was silent. The heat was blasting so high the windows had steamed. Huh, maybe sometimes hitting things with a wrench was a valid method of repair.

Trading one problem for another seemed about right. Astrid shut the door behind her and took off her shoes and coat. When she reached the kitchen, she shook Meatball's food like a maraca and waited for his nightly sprint to the kitchen but was met with only silence.

She did a thorough sweep of the apartment which took about five minutes. Her apartment would be horrible for hide and seek. Meatball must have snuck out sometime after she left. Outside the snow continued to fall. He'd be back soon enough.

She tried to read and when that didn't work, she put on music and rearranged her bookshelf. Arranging the spines in a rainbow, like that one Pinterest board Darby had shown her. It got colder and it got darker but still, Meatball didn't return.

Astrid paced her apartment, glancing out the window every so often. The snow was accumulating in mounds like someone had forgotten to say *enough cheese already.*

Finally, she threw on her coat and boots and headed outside.

ASTRID'S HANDS were frozen even inside her mittens. She'd circled the block enough times to win the Indy 500 and she was no closer to finding her cat. Panic clawed its way up from her chest and lodged at the base of her throat.

When Darby answered on the second ring her voice was hoarse. And Darby didn't sound much better. Astrid only managed to get out Meatball and missing, the nearby was explaining to her how to drop a pin.

Astrid stood in place and waited. She wasn't sure how Darby could help find Meatball, but knowing she was on her way had sparked hope in Astrid's chest. She was freezing and panicking and smiling. The human equivalent of the sun coming out during a rainstorm was on her way to help.

A red car shot down the street toward her. Astrid watched in awe as Darby did a u-turn across two lanes, fast and fabulous. She fishtailed a bit, then screeched to a halt right in front of Astrid.

Before Darby could even exit her car, a pickup truck carrying James arrived. Followed by a BMW that she was sure was Mia's even though the windows were tinted. Darby had called in the Calvary.

Darby walked over to Astrid wearing her silly Broncos pom-pom hat. In the streetlight, Astrid could see the dark circles under her eyes.

"Thanks for coming. And for bringing reinforcements."

"Of course." Darby reached out and ran her hand up and down Astrid's arm. She wanted to collapse into her touch.

"Ok." James clapped her mittens together. "What's the plan? How long has he been missing?"

"I'm, um, not sure. He was there when I left earlier but not when I got back. The guy fixing the heat didn't close my apartment door?"

"Your heat broke again?" Darby's eyebrows knit together, either in concern or to keep the snow from her eyes. "You could have called me."

Astrid nodded. "Yeah."

"So he's been missing what? A few hours? Is that unusual for him?"

"Not really, but something just feels off." Astrid crossed her arms over her chest. Was all of this just an overreaction? The wind picked up, blowing snow into her eyes and stinging her nose.

James nodded. "It's the same way with Nora for me. I get a sixth sense when something's wrong with her. I'm thinking we should split up. Mia and I will head south and you and Astrid head north."

"Do you know where he likes to hang out?"

"What, like, bars?"

"No like alleys, yards…" Mia narrowed her eyes.

"Oh, right, sorry. I'm not really sure."

"That's okay, we'll all just do our best to think like cats," James said.

"On it! He likes to hide under the bed so he's probably just hunkered down somewhere waiting out the snow. We're actually kind of lucky it's snowing." Darby smiled and nodded her head."

"Darby, I adore you, but in what world is a blizzard while we're looking for a lost cat a *good* thing?" Mia shivered and shoved her hands into her pockets.

"Because we can look for paw prints," Darby said like it was the most obvious thing in the world.

"That makes sense actually." Mia pulled her phone from her pocket. "Okay everyone, turn on location sharing and your ringer so we can find each other, too."

Darby's friends must really love her. Astrid couldn't imagine either of them were very happy with her right now and she wasn't very happy with herself either. Mia looked absolutely miserable as she and James trudged down the street. In fact, the only person who didn't look miserable was Darby. Darby looked like she was on a mission.

Darby pulled a bag of treats out of her pocket and dropped a few into her palm. "Ok, let's do this."

"Where did you get cat treats?"

"I bought some for Meatball the other day." Darby smiled in a way that didn't quite reach her eyes.

Astrid nodded and took a few steps away, emotion burning in her chest.

DARBY SHINED her phone's flashlight under a dumpster while Astrid popped the lid to look inside.

"Look, Darby, I want to say sorry for the other day."

"You don't have to be sorry." Darby's smile didn't reach her eyes. Astrid didn't think she'd ever seen her like that before.

"I was overwhelmed and rude when all you did was help me."

"You're allowed to want space, Astrid. I know I can come on strong, and what you want is casual. I pushed when I should have pulled."

"It wasn't you though, not really. It was just—" Astrid gestured broadly. "All of it. Spending time with you and your friends reminded me of everything I don't have. That I chose not to have because I wanted to protect myself. And then I met you and I wanted to be a part of your life, but at the same time I was terrified of it."

For years Astrid had been looking for a place to make her feel at home. But she'd felt more at home in that house being renovated with Darby and her friends than she had in a long time. A home that was nobody's home but also all of theirs because they were building it together. They were making something of it.

Darby seemed to be waiting for Astrid to say more, but the vulnerability was starting to fog her brain like a hangover.

"I spent the week eating the muffins you left and feeling sad."

Darby tilted her head. "How are you able to feel sad while eating muffins?"

"It's a talent."

Darby laughed and Astrid took it in like fresh air. "So, you missed me. But what are you afraid of?"

"Letting myself rely on something just to have it disappear. You're the something in that sentence."

"Gee, thanks."

"I'm not saying this right. What I mean is that I've spent so long keeping everything at arm's length and then you came out of nowhere and got so close. I could feel myself starting to count on you. My days didn't feel right until we talked, and all I could think was how sad I'd be when you moved on."

"I own my house, Astrid. I'm not going anywhere."

"You know what I mean." Astrid shoved her hands into her pockets. She wanted to run as fast as she could from this conversation and at the same time, she didn't want to leave Darby's side.

Darby stepped forward and rested her forehead against Astrid's. "I really don't."

Astrid closed her eyes, frozen in the moment. She closed her eyes and let the heat of Darby's body warm her.

"You make everything a little warmer, a little brighter. Even worried about Meatball and upset that I was such a jerk to you the other day, you still have the ability to make me feel like the sun is shining on me."

Darby pulled her head back to look into Astrid's eyes as if needing to see the sincerity there.

A poppy song started to play from Darby's coat pocket. "Come on." Darby reached for Astrid's hand and pulled it from her pocket. "I think James and Mia have news."

• • •

"So we came back because I needed something from the truck and he was just rolling around in the snow right there." James pointed to the stoop of Astrid's apartment building.

"Aw, he was making snowcats!" Darby scooped up Meatball and held him over her shoulder like a baby. She bounced slightly like she was soothing him. Maybe she was soothing herself. "Where's Mia?"

James hiked a thumb over her shoulder at Mia's car, which was running. "She said something about needing to defrost before dinner."

"Ugh, dinner sounds so good. Want to get some food?" Darby switched the cat to her other shoulder.

Astrid felt fear like an icicle in her chest at the thought of Darby leaving. But she couldn't ask her to stay. Not after basically kicking her out the other day.

"I would but I was actually supposed to meet Zee about an hour ago."

"Oh gosh, you should go. Tell her sorry and thanks for finding him. You're a Meatball hero."

"I'll never tire of your sandwich jokes, Darbara. Have a good night, I'll see you tomorrow. Bye, Astrid." James pecked Darby's cheek then nodded to Astrid before striding to her truck.

Astrid took a step closer to Darby. It might not be fair, but for the first time in a long time she knew exactly what she wanted to happen next. Astrid scratched meatball's ears.

"You should stay." Astrid rested her chin on Darby's free shoulder and rested a hand on her hip.

"To make sure Meatball's alright?"

"No. For me."

Darby leaned back against her and Astrid buried her face against Darby's neck. All around them the snow continued to fall. Astrid felt like she could stand there forever.

"Ok, but only if you're sure," Darby said.

"I'm sure. I want you here."

EPILOGUE
NINE MONTHS LATER

DARBY

"Ugh, cease and desist, Meatball."

Astrid's voice cut through Darby's dream and she cracked one eye open. "What's wrong?"

Meatball was perched on Astrid's pillow, her dark hair sticking out of his mouth.

"He won't stop grooming me."

"I think he just wants to take care of you, babe."

Astrid sighed. "Ok, that's cute, I guess. But maybe he could care for me not at the crack of dawn."

Darby glanced at the clock. "It's eight a.m. We should probably get up anyway, we have so much fun stuff to do to get ready for today."

Meatball jumped down from the bed and left the room. Darby got the feeling that their conversations bothered him.

"About that." Astrid rolled toward Darby. Her hair was a disaster. "Are you sure a party is the best idea for this announcement?"

"Of course! Don't you want to tell all our friends together?"

"I mean, I guess?"

"It's a big deal, Ash, they're going to be so happy about it."

"I just feel like you shouldn't have asked me during sex. You know I'll say yes to basically anything."

"It wasn't during sex." Darby crossed her arms over her naked chest, she was going for indignant but it was also a little cold now that the covers had slipped down. "It was a good old fashioned make out. We were fully clothed."

"Oh right," Astrid took Darby's wrist and pulled her arm away. She was giving her bedroom eyes. "That was nice. Want to show me how that goes again?" She wrapped an arm around Darby's waist and pulled their bodies together. She swept Darby's mess of curls aside. A burst of cool air quickly replaced by the gentle bite of Astrid's mouth made Darby shiver.

How was Astrid so warm?

"It was a little more than nice if I remember correctly." It was hard to form words with Astrid's tongue on her neck.

Astrid kissed along Darby's collarbone. She pressed into Astrid's mouth when she paused to leave a mark in what Darby had quickly learned was one of her favorite spots, the apex of her neck and shoulder, the one that Darby's shirts *just* about covered but not quite.

"This could be a little more than nice, too. You only need like six hours to get ready for the party, right?"

"Five if you help me."

"Deal."

Astrid rolled away from Darby, opening the drawer of her nightstand.

Darby loved all the ways of being with Astrid—walking next to her down the street or laying with her on the couch. Cuddling in bed, and dancing around each other as they made dinner in one of their kitchens.

But lately, Darby had especially loved this. Astrid finished adjusting the straps and patted her thighs. Darby straddled her, bracing her hands on Astrid's pillow.

Darby loved the way Astrid looked at her when she was on top. Reverently. She loved riding her like this, watching the way sweat shimmered on her neck, waiting for Darby's tongue

Though they'd yet to find a strap on that beat the feeling of Astrid's fingers inside her; this newest one was close. And purple, which didn't hurt its case either.

Darby loved the race of Astrid's heartbeat under her palm as she braced a hand on her chest and took her in. She rocked her hips and focused on the light sheen of sweat gathering on Astrid's forehead, while her own heartbeat kicked up as the effervescent feeling low in her stomach steadily built.

Darby leaned forward trying to get more friction and Astrid reached her hand between their bodies, running her fingers lightly over Darby's clit, focusing a bit longer on that spot just below where she liked it.

"Wait, let me look at you."

Darby's breasts brushed against Astrid's. The contact made her gasp as she began to unwind. As her orgasm grew, she brought her mouth to Astrid's neck, all tongue and teeth and lips. Leaving a mark of her own.

"Can you explain to me again why we're having the party at my small apartment and not your house?" Astrid was leaning against the kitchen counter.

Darby's hands were about as frosted as the confetti cupcakes in front of her. Cupcakes were one of the wonders of the world. They went into the oven as amorphous goo and emerged fully formed like little butterflies. Anyway, Astrid had a point, and it wasn't as though she hadn't considered having the party at her house. She'd been considering it for the past hour as she found creative ways to invent counter space in Astrid's kitchen. She was particularly proud of the cutting board she'd set over an open drawer.

"Because it's really important to me that Meatball is present for the announcement. I think all of our friends will want to see him too."

"Of course. Speaking of Meatball, have you seen him lately?"

"Yeah, he's sleeping in his hammock."

Astrid squinted at Darby. "When did he get a hammock?"

"When I bought him one a few weeks ago." She grinned at Astrid. "Will you taste this? I'm not sure if it needs more sugar."

Astrid took a few steps toward her. "Isn't it, like, all sugar?"

"Mostly." She shrugged.

Astrid leaned in to taste and Darby truly tried her best to resist smearing vanilla frosting on her face, but some impulses were simply impossible to deny.

Darby moved quickly, swerving her hand out of the path of Astrid's mouth, leaving a vivid streak of frosting across her cheek.

"I literally just finished getting ready, babe." Astrid sighed dramatically, but her crooked grin told a different story.

Darby leaned forward and kissed her cheek, darting her tongue out to taste the frosting. "On second thought, the frosting is perfect."

Astrid grabbed a towel and threw it at Darby. "You are so weird, I love it."

"I know." Darby felt the warm glow of Astrid's words in her chest. Astrid never seemed to tire of her. She seemed to relish her personality rather than endure it. And to Darby, that felt better than just about anything.

"Do you want me to take over here so you can go get dressed before your friends get here? Are we supposed to wear the shirts you made everyone?" Astrid pinched the hem of her black t-shirt.

"No, I don't want to ruin the surprise." Darby licked a bit more frosting from Astrid's face. "Once you finish frosting them, can you write on them? I left a diagram of what I want it to look like."

Astrid studied the sheet of paper laid out on the counter and then narrowed her eyes at Darby. "I'm not sure frosting calligraphy is realistic."

"Just do cursive then." Darby gave Astrid a quick kiss on the cheek on her way out of the kitchen.

DARBY HAD JUST STEPPED into her jumpsuit when she heard Astrid greeting James and Zee at the door. Mia and Lauryn followed a few moments later. *Okay, almost showtime.*

She lingered in the bedroom listening to Astrid's easy banter with her friends. She loved hearing them laugh together. At first, Darby had felt like the glue holding their extended friendship together, but just last week Astrid and James had ordered Chinese food and put together a new dresser for her room. The very same dresser that Darby was now the proud owner of two point five drawers in.

Astrid excused herself to get everyone drinks and Darby's curiosity won out. She cracked the door to eavesdrop on her friends. Keeping the reason for the party to herself had basically been torture, but she'd dug deep and found reserves of willpower she didn't know she possessed.

James stood with her hand on Zee's back. Zee's black hair nearly swept against James' fingers as they traced circles along her spine. Mia and Lauryn stood facing them. Mia's raven hair was center-parted and flawless while Lauryn's sat in a messy, yet somehow chic, pile of dark curls on top of her head. Darby patted down her own messy hair and removed a stray bit of frosting.

They were beautiful together, her friends and their partners.

Though only Lauryn had observed Darby's requested dress code of onesie casual. Their loss. Darby shimmied her jumpsuit over her hips. Only masochists still wore real jeans.

"So what do you think the announcement is?" Mia asked the group.

Darby felt excitement well up in her chest. Watching her friends from out of view felt like playing hide and seek—she had that giddy feeling that always came with hearing the seeker's footsteps. Darby always had to fight the impulse to give herself away.

"I mean, there are champagne flutes and cupcakes over there." Zee tilted her head toward the sideboard in the dining area. "My money's on engagement."

"Damn, Astrid locked that down fast." Lauryn nodded her agreement.

"No way." James shook her head. "The cupcakes and the glasses are just Darby; I don't think we can read too much into those. Besides, they don't even live together."

"Yeah, no way it's an engagement, not enough glitter. But not because they don't live together. I think they both just like their space. There's nothing wrong with that." Mia swept her hair over one shoulder.

Lauryn turned to her. "How do you know it's not an engagement then?"

"Because secrets are Darby's kryptonite, especially big, happy news." James moved her arm to wrap around Zee's hip. "Remember when she blew my big surprise for you?"

"I wouldn't say she blew it." Zee laughed. "More like softened the ground."

"I don't know," Lauryn said. "I think we're about to see a rock."

"Darby's not that into jewelry. Might be like an engagement friendship bracelet or something. Like the ones she made us, Mia."

"Or engagement sunglasses? I'm thinking heart frames lined with rhinestones." Mia grinned.

"Ok, I actually love that." Lauryn said. "Do you think they make those?"

"I'll look for them, Laur."

Darby swept out of the bedroom just as Astrid returned from the kitchen with a tray of champagne flutes.

"Oh hey, Darbs." Mia pulled her into a hug.

Followed by Lauryn, then James, and finally Zee. She squeezed each of them in turn. Despite Darby repeatedly advocating for group hugs, her friends were traditionalists.

Astrid came to a stop next to Darby, and she began passing around the glasses.

"Your jumpsuit is super cute, babe," Astrid said. She brushed her lips against Darby's ear.

"Totally cute." Mia agreed. "But I'm not used to seeing you in black."

"Astrid picked it out for me. Shall we do a toast?"

"What are we toasting to, Darbara?" James accepted a glass.

"And why are we doing it with champagne flutes full of gummy bears?" Mia wrinkled her nose and sniffed. "Peach gummy bears at that."

"They're champagne gummy bears." Darby could feel the excitement thrumming in her chest.

"My apologies, Darbs. Of course they are." Mia bit back a smile.

"It's a special occasion. Excuse me for being fancy." Darby laughed, the announcement like bubbles on the tip of her tongue. "Let's toast to the future and friendship and found families."

"Here, here!" Lauryn said.

"Okay." James nodded. "How did you envision this toast going?"

Darby pinched a gummy bear from the top of her glass and held it aloft. Astrid and Lauryn followed suit. Mia and Zee were the last to raise their bears.

"Okay, now they meet in the middle." Darby extended her arm toward the center of their impromptu circle and the others followed her lead.

And in the world's cutest toast, they tapped their bears together and ate them.

"Those are better than I thought they'd be," Mia said. "Are there actual drinks, too? And when can we hear the big news?"

"Maybe when Meatball wakes up from his nap?" Darby glanced over her shoulder at the hammock. One of Meatball's striped legs hung over the side.

"Really, babe?" Astrid rested her chin on Darby's shoulder. "Let's just tell them."

"Yes, please tell us!" Lauryn clapped her hands together.

"Okay fine, but if he's upset later, I'm telling Meatball that I was peer pressured."

Mia hummed in agreement. "We're okay with that."

Darby wrapped her arm around Astrid's waist and pulled her close. The bubbly feeling had migrated to her chest. "Astrid and I—" she shot one more look at Meatball's sleeping form. He'd recover.

"You and Astrid what?" Zee sounded exasperated, but she was leaning on James, balanced on the balls of her feet.

"We've decided it's time to adopt Meatball. Officially."

Her friends were quiet for a moment. And then another.

"Oh my gosh, are you serious?" James asked.

"We registered him earlier today, and he got microchipped, too." Astrid smiled her crooked smile, and Darby's heart felt ready to spill over.

"I wanted you all to formally meet Meatball Darby-West."

"This is really great news, you two." James blinked back tears from her eyes and Zee put a reassuring hand on her shoulder.

"Thanks." Astrid placed a kiss on the top of Darby's head and she leaned into it. "That's what the cupcakes say, but they're not entirely legible."

Mia wandered over to the sideboard and studied the tray of cupcakes. White frosting topped with orange lettering. "These look like how I sign my name on a touchscreen."

Darby nodded. "They're cursive."

"Anyway, we've got plenty of food and some party gifts I want everyone to put on."

"Not again," James said.

"Do I finally get a Darby shirt?" Lauryn grinned. "I've been coveting Mia's since the Super Bowl.

"Yep! You get a Meatball Sub shirt, and you get a Meatball Sub shirt!" Darby pointed to her friends and did her best Oprah impression.

She turned to Astrid. "Will you grab Meatball while I get the shirts?"

"Sure, but why?"

Darby lowered her voice and leaned closer to Astrid. "For the group photo. I was thinking we could use it on the holiday card. Unless you think I'm being too much?"

"No, babe, I think you're the perfect amount of you."

THE END

THANK YOU!

Thank you for reading The Bright Side! I appreciate it so much! The support of readers is what keeps me writing.

Keep reading to find the first two chapters of Must Love Silence.

ABOUT THE FLIPPIN' FANTASTIC ROMANCE SERIES

This three-book series was a collaboration with Stephanie Shea and Bryce Oakley.

Three best friends, three novellas. Meet James, Mia, and Darby, the women behind Flippin' Fantastic Renovations.

Each novella explores one of the friends' love stories, but all are grounded by their friendship.

James is the handyma'am of the crew. She knows her way around a power tool but not a conversation with Zee the beautiful, if pesky, next-door neighbor.

Mia could sell a beach house in Idaho. She might be all pristine suits and sharp heels, but she loves fiercely. Can she get through working with their newest client Lauryn while protecting her heart? Or will the heat of their attraction melt her defenses?

Darby loves throwing pillows and parties. She believes each day is what you make it. Astrid is waiting for things to be perfect before committing to anything, including a full wardrobe. Can Darby's heart sunglasses help her see the bright side?

Each book can be read as a standalone, but just like with friends, they're better when they're together.

- The Bright Side by Lucy Bexley

- Against the Grain by Bryce Oakley

- Collide by Stephanie Shea

NO STRINGS

Lucy Bexley

NO STRINGS
PREVIEW

SYNOPSIS

Fun is the one thing **Elsie Webb** takes seriously. Though she'd be having a lot more of it if Haelstrom Media paid her enough to actually get out of debt. She's determined to hold out on contract negotiations for her kids' television show Fangley Heights until she gets what she deserves. There's only one problem, the head of the network just died and left her future more uncertain than ever.

Forty-eight hours and one funeral–that's all **Jones Haelstrom** has to get through before she can return to her life in LA that's as ordered and sparse as an IKEA showroom. When she steps in as CEO of her father's media company, Elsie Webb is her first problem to deal with. Elsie ends up challenging Jones in ways she never could have predicted, starting with an attraction neither can avoid.

As their attraction teeters on the edge of something more both agree to keep it casual. A no-strings agreement and disclosure to HR should be enough to keep things between Jones and Elsie from getting tangled, right?

CHAPTER ONE
ELSIE

Was hitting someone with a puppet technically assault? Elsie's mind said yes, but her heart—and hopefully a jury— said no. She didn't want to risk hurting the star of the show, even if he was made of felt. Not to mention, that bundle of fabric and stuffing kept a roof over her head. Elsie grimaced. She didn't really think of Fangley like that—he was a more realized person than half of her colleagues.

The set of her show Fangley Heights was gearing up for a day of filming and Elsie was already nearing her limit.

"Stop trying to control the puppet. Relax. Let *it* control you."

Elsie cringed as Trey's hand came to rest on her shoulder like a small, hot pancake, lingering for a few scorching seconds before it slid off. Trey used his hypnotist's voice, something he'd learned from one of his afternoon acting workshops. Soft and wispy and boring as hell.

Elsie had to admit it was effective. Talking to Trey did make her want to pass out to escape any further interaction with him. His personality was a constant interruption. It was like he couldn't resist talking when she was trying to focus. Her entire job was to control puppets, and he was trying to make it into some kind of metaphorical, New Age thing instead of what it was: skillful manipulation. These puppets didn't even have strings.

As the nephew of the Haelstrom's second in charge, Trey was the network's golden boy even though Elsie carried the show and frankly, she was reaching her limit with being anyone's second choice. And okay, so maybe there was that one time she had insulted some 'important' sponsors by comparing their conversation to oyster crackers that have been in an old woman's purse since the Great Depression. So dry she was left choking on their dust. But still, people didn't give second chances anymore? Was it too late to stick a stipulation in her contract for next season that Trey's puppet, Smirch, would meet an untimely end? To date, giving Trey's puppet the worst possible name was her proudest accomplishment. Even if it was technically her roommate, Avery, who had come up with it during a particularly intense game of Jenga.

Elsie took a deep breath to keep from laughing at the memory of Avery knocking over the tower in exuberance when the name occurred to them. She checked her monitor as she raised her right arm over her head and above the small wall in front of her. One thing they don't tell you about puppeteering is, it makes your shoulders look great. Like seriously ripped. Well, mostly just the one shoulder, but still they should put that in the drama school brochure. Maybe she could contribute that tidbit so they'd stop asking her for money, which they absolutely knew she didn't have.

"I think if you just loosen your wrist, you could—"

Elsie sliced her gaze at Trey.

His warm whisper washed over her face and she shuddered. With her headset over her ears, she couldn't hear most of what he was saying, a small mercy, but the fact that she could see a bit of sweat on his forehead made his proximity vaguely threatening. What she'd like to do was control him. She'd donate him to Goodwill.

Elsie glanced back down at her monitor. Trey's fingers seared her skin as they wound around her wrist. His new gold watch jangled. She added 'demand a raise' to her running mental list of contract negotiation points. Elsie had a good feeling that all she had to do to get all the stipulations she wanted was to hold out for a few more days. The network would cave, she just knew it.

She took a deep breath and lowered her headset. "Are you trying to derail my entire process?"

"You just looked like you needed my help keeping this little guy steady." Trey reached up to touch Fangley. *Nobody* touched Elsie's puppet. She flicked her wrist so Fangley's hand smacked Trey's forehead before he had the chance. He blinked at her but made no move to call the authorities. So hitting someone annoying with a puppet technically wasn't assault, just as she'd suspected.

Rebecca, the showrunner, poked her head through the studio door and called Trey over. Elsie felt the tension drain out of her. Even Fangley's shoulders relaxed.

Elsie used the momentary peace to ready herself for the scene they were filming that afternoon, the one where Fangley and his cat sidekick, Ratatouille, put on way too much makeup in an attempt to fit in. The beautiful thing about the show was that its connection to reality could be tenuous as long as the bits were engaging. For example, why would a blue-tinted young vampire like Fangley and his Maine Coon sidekick think doing a full clown face of makeup would make them *less* conspicuous? Either way, she was looking forward to the arrival of Gabby, Ratatouille's handler.

The Fangley universe worked on a perfect kind of logic: very little of it.

Fangley Heights was in its third year of production. Most days Elsie couldn't believe her luck. She had picked essentially the most unemployable major, despite her father's desire for her to do something respectable. What he really meant was something with a high earning potential. Her father saw money as a down payment toward happiness, but he always forgot about the mortgage. Elsie had found no correlation between respectability and the size of her bank account. Quite the opposite, actually. Besides, she literally couldn't do math or handle bills. Even calculating tips was beyond her. On the other hand, the idea of saving people made something catch in her chest. So business and medicine were out. Her father wanted her to be employable. She wanted to be happy. But on *Fangley Heights*, most days she was both. Now if only everyone she'd ever met would stop making weird jokes about her being a puppeteer. At the very least bad jokes should be original.

But there wouldn't be a job, puppeteer or otherwise, if she couldn't get next season's agreement worked out. With each contractless day she barreled closer to an uncertain future.

She'd pushed her luck in negotiations, but why shouldn't she be better compensated? Fangley was her intellectual property, even if Haelstrom Media owned the trademark. Though it felt hard to say where everything would land with that in light of Hunter Haelstrom's recent passing. That little vamp went all the way back to a web series she'd done to kill the time she should have spent memorizing Hamlet in grad school. A little something productive to assuage her guilt over wasting time.

Her classmates tried to dismiss children's television as fluff, but this wasn't Punch and Judy hour. *Fangley Heights* had depth. It had whimsy with slightly charred edges. It only barely made sense. It was a show about an orphan vampire being fostered by a family in Brooklyn—a true American story. When Haelstrom Media had reached out to her just before graduation, she couldn't believe her luck. Elsie had felt so sure signing that contract would be her golden ticket, but she was young and naive. She didn't understand sub-clauses and percentages or that one paragraph they always threw in that stipulated media appearance requirements.

Maybe they'd learned their lesson after her season one sponsor disaster. She wished now she'd read that contract, committed every line to memory. Been asked to do a series of complicated crosswords before signing it. But she hadn't, because this was back when she still trusted people to do the right thing. She thought she'd pay off her loans, buy an apartment, and stop worrying about getting by. And yet, they were wrapping up season three and she was still sharing a place with Avery. Treating themselves meant the fancy two-for-one egg roll special.

Elsie was struggling, even though her character was a cultural icon to kids everywhere who were still learning to tie their shoelaces. Fangley was a celebrity. If a puppet could be a celeb. What was she saying? *Of course* a puppet could be famous. Oscar the Grouch? Rizzo? Iconic. Plus, as a nine-year-old vampire desperate to fit in, Fangley was relatable. For the pun-filled *Make-Over-Done* episode, Elsie had spent a solid week working with their local designer and props team on *Drag Fangley*, as she'd been thinking of him. He looked almost frightening this way, just this side of familiar, like a woman in a facemask. A ghoul you could trust.

Elsie studied Fangley and wondered if she should have let the costume department and designers just craft a mask for him. They had made some latex prototypes to mimic a cold cream and blush treatment, but they all looked too much like meringue, the cold cream mask crested in waves. And when Elsie had done a run-through of the scenes with Fangley and the mask, none of his expressions had been visible. Which upped the creep factor considerably past the tolerance of their kindergarten focus group.

The creation of a new Fangley had set them back several weeks and Rebecca warned they were approaching a meeting-with-the-boss level of being behind schedule. All of that was up-in-the-air now with the new boss still being uncertain. But Elsie had a good feeling about today. The "makeup" could be layered on individually to the new version of Fangley; she had the blush and eyelashes lined up on a table behind the wall of the set. Everything was ready to stick on Fangley's ghastly face. They'd be taking a Mr. Potato Head approach. There was probably a merchandising opportunity here, not that she was giving those ideas away to Haelstrom Media for free anymore. Elsie was still waiting to see any income from her point zero five percent share of sales from trademarked Fangley merchandise.

Elsie set about her pre-rehearsal routine. The choreography of puppets was intense. Like synchronized swimming, or one of those two-piece horse costumes. Reliably, Elsie was the ass of their outfit. In this week's episode, Amanda was playing Fangley's next-door neighbor and Trey was playing Fangley's nemesis, the elementary school's suspicious science teacher. A perfect role because it was easy for Elsie and Fangley to get into the mindset of hating him.

Elsie racked her body over the foam roller, extending her back and listening to it creak and pop as she raised her arms over her head. They had an area off to the side of the set for the explicit purpose of working out the kinks that came with contorting their bodies into puppeteering postures. Sometimes it took hours after a shoot for the stiffness in Elsie's torso to fade to tolerable. She brought her hands to the ground, bracing into a wheel shape. There was a whiff of the medieval about modern-day self-care; facial peels, cooking yourself in the sun, stretching your body over a cylinder until it gave way with a series of satisfying cracks. Torture therapy.

Elsie stood slowly, like she was being raised to standing. She punched in her code and freed Fangley from his case. The puppets sitting in a row in their glass enclosures, like little lockers, reminded Elsie of babies in a hospital nursery. Tempting to snatch but constantly monitored.

Elsie set Fangley on the fake stone wall as she considered his outfit. In an increasingly routine bout of interference, the network had insisted on Fangley wearing his black cape even though that made no sense if he was trying to fit in. Everyone knew Fangley preferred to only wear his cape at home, it was a comfort item, like a blanket. But there was concern from 'certain sectors of the market' that kids were forgetting that Fangley was a vampire because the show was doing too good a job of humanizing him. Even though vampires are human, technically. Though in this case, everyone's a puppet.

The door to the fake brownstone creaked open, and out stepped Trey. His conversation with Rebecca must have been brief for him to already be back on set; Elsie hadn't realized they'd finished talking already. So much for her break.

Now she was left to wonder how long Trey had been there, silently observing her? Add that to the list of things it was better to never know. Maybe the network should be more concerned about humanizing Trey.

He hopped down the stairs from the front door to the stage and clicked his heels. In her head, Elsie watched a fantasy of him slipping on a banana peel. Ah, the power of imagination.

"So are we going to do this scene, Els? I've got a good feeling about this afternoon."

"I always come to work, Trey."

"As long as you don't throw a fit about outfits again." He reached for Elsie's shoulder but pulled his hand back as though her arm had been replaced with a bear trap. So, he had the ability to read body language after all.

"Having an opinion isn't throwing a fit. Are you going to throw a fit about your lines?" Trey's secondary character, Myrtle, was slated to be roped in by Fangley to help fix his makeup disaster in time for the spelling bee.

"No self-respecting ten-year-old girl would go along with Fangley's makeover plan."

"As someone who was once a ten-year-old girl, I can confirm that they're usually not very self-respecting."

Elsie breathed a sigh of relief as the director walked onto the set. The official signal that filming was about to start. Only Trey could be less annoying playing an evil puppet named Smirch than as himself.

THEY WERE deep into filming the second scene, the one with Trey's character, when he tripped over Elsie's not-at-all outstretched leg and they had to pause for the day. As they broke and the crew brought Trey ice, Rebecca waved Elsie over to the production control room.

This would be a good opportunity to get Rebecca's advice on her contract woes. Though the way her forehead was doing a Shar-Pei impression gave Elsie pause. Maybe she could see if the props department still had some of that cold cream from *Drag Fangley* on hand.

"So, I've got some bad news." Rebecca gave her a tight smile.

"Okay." *Shit.* "Is everything alright with Fangley?"

"Yes, of course. He's a puppet." Rebecca looked at Elsie like she was ridiculous for caring about the vampire that was literally keeping them both in a job. Millions of people cared about Fangley. He even had his own fan club: The Fangers. Not a name she would have chosen, but the fanbase of five-year-olds were not to be swayed.

"I just got word from the network, and well, you're aware that Hunter Haelstorm passed away last week, right?"

"Yes, it's very unfortunate." Elsie nodded. It was one of those things that was sad in the *royal we* sense but not necessarily upsetting to her personally.

Rebecca shrugged. "He was in his 80s and never once looked me in the eye."

"Okay, so marginally sad. I assume some people are very upset. I didn't really know him, aside from the name on my check. Do you have any idea who's taking over? Have you heard anything?"

"I'm pretty sure the will named his widow. I've only met her once, at the Christmas party two years ago, but I got the sense she wasn't a fan of the work we do here on the Heights. Did you meet her there?"

"Oh, I think I was sick that day." Elsie shrugged. She probably had been sick—sick of absolutely everything going on at work. "Do you think she'll change the show? I mean, she wouldn't, right? The numbers are good and growing each year, but I don't trust Stu for a second not to try to oust us."

Rebecca raised her hands. "I don't have any information. I know these things aren't always logical. We should take every opportunity to make sure she knows how amazing this show is. And I think it's in our best interest to get this season wrapped this week even if it means spending a few nights together. I don't want Stu to see even the tiniest window to give this show to Trey."

"I don't mind pulling all-nighters, but you know I have a no-overnights-with-Trey policy." Elsie shuddered. "Besides, who will get Trey an air cast? He might even lose the leg."

"I've never met anyone who applies soccer foul performances to real life. Once I saw him get a paper cut and fall to the ground asking for stitches."

Elsie caught the gleam in Rebecca's eye. She almost never let loose on Trey. Rebecca was in her 50s and the consummate professional. At work, anyway. Rebecca at Chewy's, the bar down the street, was a delightful person to spend time hating things with.

Elsie wiped a tear of laughter from her eye and took a deep breath. She loved mean Rebecca. Was there anything more soul-nourishing than shit talk? "I'm so sad I missed that. Next time keep the camera running. We can add it to his showreel. Maybe get him some more dramatic roles."

"Noted." Rebecca's face sobered. "I think it's critical for everyone to sign and lock in their contracts. Please tell me you're not still dragging your feet on yours." Rebecca looked at Elsie like she was going to explain why she wasn't mad, just disappointed.

Elsie grimaced.

"I mean it about your contract, Elsie. You need to sign."

"Signing it is me saying it's okay to treat me this way. To underpay me while making a killing off of my ideas." Elsie's last contract draft had been an offer so laughably low that she'd used it to sop up her spilled Lucky Charms milk.

She had *created* the show, and yet every year it felt like she was begging them to pay her enough to buy fresh vegetables. The fact that an apple in Manhattan went for ten dollars was beside the point. Then again, wasn't some money better than no money at all? That's what Avery would tell her. *Just keep us in bubble bath and bubble tea, babe.* Maybe if the show went up a little and met her halfway she could consider maybe, possibly, signing her name on the dotted line. Which was always a solid line, actually.

"I know you wanted to hold out for more money, and I think they're ready to meet you at..." Rebecca glanced at her iPad. "Seven percent below your ask. I'd take it if I were you."

All wavering drained from Elsie. *Seven percent BELOW her ask?* Were they absolutely fucking with her? Last week it was five percent. She planted her feet. Absolutely fuck that. "That's a worse offer than before. How much below Trey's ask are you advising him to take?"

"Even if I had all the details, *which I don't,* you know I can't discuss the specifics of other people's contracts." Rebecca's eyes flitted to the monitor in the control room that showed Trey sitting on the floor holding ice on his ankle and scrolling through his phone.

"Right, because telling me how much I'm being screwed would be grossly unfair to you and the network." Elsie turned to leave. She had an overwhelming desire for this day to end.

Rebecca caught her arm. "Look, just think about it, okay? This show matters so much to all of us. I don't want to see your dream crumble."

But Elsie *had* thought about it. Fangley Heights was her baby. The only thing she'd ever invested herself in fully. But if she could love something she created this much, who was to say she couldn't do it again? She thought about the notebook on her desk, full of half-finished sketches and jokes that brought tears to her eyes. That had always been her barometer for good ideas—what reaction they sparked in her. If she didn't find her own jokes funny, why would anyone else?

Elsie pushed open the door. "Trust me, Rebecca, this is far from my only dream." The door clattered behind her. If drama school had taught her anything, it was the power of a dramatic exit.

CHAPTER TWO
JONES

Jones was late. Her mother, Birdie, loved to say that she herself had never been late a day in her life, because there's no such thing as being late when you run the show, though Jones had a distinct memory of waiting until dusk for Birdie to pick her up after school. Watching the parking lot next to the playground empty until it was just her and Carl, the janitor. (Yes, as a child she'd spent enough time with the school janitor to be on a first-name basis.) Those were the days that Birdie claimed school simply ended earlier than expected.

Jones had inherited a lot of things, but her mother's brazen disregard for others wasn't among them. Jones was late because she didn't want any part of where she was headed. That, and she was currently responsible for another very small human who walked in slow motion. And it was probably even more important for her to be on time now that she was the one in charge of her father's company, however temporarily. She needed to give the impression that it might be permanent, otherwise no one would take her seriously.

After the funeral, Jones' stepmother had booked herself a few days at the spa. It felt so weird to Jones to call someone eleven years younger her stepmother. When Charity asked for time to herself, Jones had wanted to be annoyed, but she understood that Charity was facing a life much different from the one she'd had a week ago. If Birdie had taught her anything, it was that mothers didn't have to be selfless. Sometimes the very act of being selfish, knowing what you needed and taking it, was the thing that made us better to those we care about. So Jones had said she'd stay with her father's child. Well, his other child. Her brother—she needed to get used to saying that. Even if it was just until Charity got back from her mud baths and mourning. Only three days to go, or closer to two depending on what time Charity got back on Saturday for Bentley's birthday. And then Jones could go back to her life. Back to only caring for herself. She'd pick up right where she left off, reviewing the new thousand-dollar snail serum in every A-lister's virtual cart. She could feel the hydrating benefits already.

The city sky gave a roll of thunder. Though it could have been a building being demolished. Both equally common occurrences. Actually, the city probably had more demolition dust storms than actual storms.

Jones glanced down to check on Bentley to make sure she'd remembered his rain jacket but he was gone. Children are like assassins, most dangerous when they're silent. She stopped in the middle of the sidewalk. Other pedestrians on West 42nd streamed around her; one gentleman cross-checked her and knocked her bag to the ground. Apparently Mr. Hockey Moves had places to be, but he could have looked a little less smug about it. Jones shook it off. It wasn't like she was a tourist, even if she technically hadn't lived here in close to two decades. She retrieved her bag then widened her stance to withstand further attempts to trample her as she spun around slowly and scanned her surroundings.

Jones had been in charge for three days and she'd already lost her brother. She'd never realized panic was a thing she could taste—it sat like battery acid in the back of her throat.

She was looking for a small child dressed like an executive on his yacht. Chinos, boat shoes, one of those little belts with the whales on it—or was it lobsters? Either way, some sort of sea dweller she'd never mess with. One might think this look to be distinctive, but in Midtown it was yuppie camo. When it came to dressing him, she'd done the best with the options available to her. It wasn't just their thirty-seven-year age gap that was making this weird. At over forty, Jones had decided long ago that kids were not in her future. And now, everyone from the cashier at the bodega where she bought milk for her coffee that morning, to the owner of the florist for her father's memorial kept referring to Bentley as her son. Most times, she didn't have the energy to explain the intricacies of their modern family. It was, in a word, a mindfuck.

Jones spotted his tiny figure dressed in an absurdly expensive Day-Glo sweater crouched on the sidewalk half a block back. She released a sharp exhale of relief. What was he—oh god he was picking up a piece of gum. Kids had immune systems of Teflon, right? Or at least city kids did. Honestly, for something Bentley could pick up off of a street in Manhattan, gum was pretty tame and unlikely to be lethal.

She walked back into the rushing stream of oncoming pedestrians and squatted down next to him. "Hey, buddy, can you stay with me?"

He looked up at her with the same slate blue eyes as her own, and it was then that she noticed he was chewing on something. Crunching, really, the sound as one with the jackhammer one avenue over. They really would be putting her immune system theory to the test.

Why would anyone leave a child in her care? Even if she had agreed, a few days was a few days too long.

Jones held out her hand for her brother's, but instead of reaching for it he leaned forward and spit into it. Gum, hard as a flattened penny landed in her palm. This was one for the books. Jones Haelstrom, kneeling on a city street with a palmful of spit and fossilized gum. She threw it into the oncoming traffic like a grenade.

What would Birdie have to say about this? *It's New York, if you're not eccentric there, you're not alive.*

Eccentric and in need of a shower. Oh, right, and really fucking late for this meeting with Haelstrom Media's lawyers.

Jones looked down at her knees. She was in the dress she'd worn to the funeral a few days before. For some reason, she'd expected to go back home to California shortly after the burial, before whatever this new interminable situation was. But what else could she do except offer to stay when Charity said she planned to leave Bentley with his nanny? *You could have gone straight to JFK and boarded a flight home,* Birdie's voice in her head supplied helpfully. Jones had agreed to stay, and now she was stuck like gum to the sidewalk, getting walked all over, while Charity was mummifying herself in a mixture of kelp and clay.

Jones scraped her palm on the concrete and stood.

She grabbed Bentley's hand and tried very hard not to think about why it was sticky.

THE BUILDING's lobby had a mausoleum quality, all smooth white stone and echoes of ghosts. The double-height ceiling stretched upward, drawing her eye to a banner that hung above the gold elevators. It was a tapestry portrait, faded in the sun, so that the man's tie was now a magenta, but she'd know those icy eyes anywhere. Her father stared back at her like some sort of larger-than-life communist propaganda. Welcoming. Humbling. Deeply unsettling.

He had always considered himself above others.

The security guard glanced at her ID and waved her through. His generic black suit and the clear wire dangling along his neck like an errant curl, brought to mind a secret service agent. Well, even if the security was lax, he at least seemed prepared for secret comms about lunch deliveries. *The Eagle's chicken caesar wrap has landed.*

She knotted her free hand around the strap of her bag. On her other side, Bentley swayed repeatedly against her leg, knocking her off balance in her heels. How could three days create a year's worth of exhaustion? And why the hell was she wearing heels? Right, because she'd only brought one other pair of shoes, and they were her favorite slip-ons, which she loved too much to put them through the marble and meetings and misery of this day. Plus, without her father around, there was no one to get a rise out of by dressing down like she had when she'd interned for him in college.

For the first time in her life, Jones had under-packed. The call that her father had passed came in the middle of the night, and she'd thrown a few things in a carry-on. She figured she'd buy something somber in New York and take the first return flight she could find after a reasonably respectful amount of time. Say, twelve hours after his funeral. She'd definitely planned to be back for work on Monday. And, well, it was *a Monday*. And this was technically work. Only instead of returning to the silly little lifeforce-draining lifestyle articles her editor gave her about green juices purifying the soul, she was in a cold Manhattan lobby re-wearing her funeral clothes. Not that Jones would turn down a super fruit soul cleanse herself about now, such was the weakness of her resolve in that moment.

The elevator doors slid shut, and Jones met her own gaze in the mirrored surface. The doors had a slightly wavy effect, like a carnival funhouse where no one exits feeling good about themselves. It was like she was gazing at her future self, and that self was…exhausted. And oddly puffy. If she didn't find a place in New York that sold vegetables instead of bagels, she wouldn't survive the week.

Bentley wriggled his hand free and smashed a few extra buttons. *Perfect.*

They'd be taking the scenic route.

What was a few more minutes? When you're late you're late. And Bentley pressing buttons meant he wasn't eating street gum. Maybe she was starting to understand parents who were chill amid the chaos. She leaned back against the wall, taking some pressure off her feet. These heels were the devil's vise.

Bentley's reflection loomed. He was a captain of chaos, a titan of terror. He could pass for a boy CEO of a startup, heading to a meeting with an angel investor. Jones wished she'd thought to dress down as a power move. His look said *money matters to me but impressing you doesn't*, and frankly, Jones would be trying to channel that energy for the next hour of her life. She *hoped* this meeting didn't take more than an hour. She still needed to figure out dinner, and Bentley kept rejecting her salad options. Even the ones with exciting things like sunflower seeds or blueberries. Kids were impossible.

THE STUDIO WAS STILL BRIGHT, even though it was mostly deserted. A few people lingered near a small set, including a woman wearing a headset and arranging a jumble of stuffed animals.

Behind her, a throat cleared. Every muscle in Jones' neck locked.

"Ms. Haelstrom?"

A man with an egg-shaped head and a wreath of hair extended his hand. When he moved, his head gleamed brightly in the lights. "Stu Winkle, I'm not sure if you remember me. Do you still go by Joanie?"

Jones freed her hand from Bentley's and placed it in Stu's. He very nearly stifled his grimace as she transferred a bit of stickiness. Oh yes, she definitely remembered this guy. When she was a kid, he once offered her candy that was so warm from his pocket, the thought of it still made her gag. By the time she'd interned here during her senior year, his offers had been a lot more suggestive, though equally gross. Still, as much as she might find him distasteful, she couldn't just ignore her father's right-hand man, at least not while he was partially in charge of Haelstrom Media.

"Of course, Stu, good to see you still making people uncomfortable in the workplace. You can call me Jones." He kept shaking her hand until she pulled it from his grasp. Another maneuver she'd borrowed from Bentley.

Stu laughed like he was in on some joke between them. "Come on now, I was just being welcoming."

Jones ignored him. After her years of dealing with Stu and not wanting to annoy her dad, it felt nice to finally speak her mind. She squatted down. "Bentley, how about you go over there and play with the toys?"

Bentley took off running, his little boat shoes squeaking on the floor. Stu reached out a hand as though to pull the boy back.

Jones shot Stu an amused look. "Sorry, I probably should have asked first. Is that okay? I mean I could always bring him to the meeting."

Stu's face sobered at the mention of Bentley in the board-room. "Oh no, this is perfect. Fangley Heights babysits kids after school every day. It's their bread and butter. I'll just fire off a quick text, and someone will be here to watch him in just a minute."

She followed Stu to the door, but when he held it open with half his body blocking it, she stayed back. Jones wasn't exactly large, but she was an adult and there was no way her hips were getting through that space without him "acciden-tally" brushing against her. No thank you. The silence stretched as they both waited for the other to break and move first. Jones nodded at him, and after another moment he pushed the door wide and shuffled through. She'd hold her own door with two broken arms to avoid the feeling she was getting from him. Jones had gotten enough slime on her from the gum incident already. And she'd had enough actual contact on their walk from the train to last her a lifetime. Only the F train could make her miss the 405. At least in LA, accidental contact looked like being rear-ended.

Jones followed Stu through the labyrinth of hallways, her nervous energy ricocheting in her chest like a lightning bug trapped in a jar. Everything looked so different from when she'd interned here all those years ago, Haelstrom Media had moved up in the world both in terms of cultural cache and by two whole floors in this building. She fought the impulse to run and instead slowed to let herself fall a few paces behind. Her eyes scanned the gleaming white floors. She expected to see a trail of slimy footprints in the shape of his loafers, but they just let out a pitiful little dog toy squeak. If only she knew where she was going, she could excuse herself and find a restroom or a quiet corner to take a few deep breaths and center herself. She did a quick safety check for an exit sign and locked eyes with a woman who was watching them with an amused expression on her face.

The woman's gaze drifted over Jones appraisingly. Jones felt the heat of her green eyes like the sun on her skin. So maybe not amused. *But interested?*

Jones looked down at her weird funeral clothes. Okay, interest was unlikely. Maybe she was just sizing Jones up as the new boss. Jones straightened to her best boss height, which was just her real height, but more serious.

Jones watched as the woman raked her fingers through her shoulder-length brown hair, sweeping it to one side so that her curls shot out erratically. It was wavy in an uneven way that reminded Jones of finally letting her hair down at the end of the night. Sweet relief. The freedom of no one left to impress.

Though, if Jones was being honest, the woman had an air

of not wanting to impress at all. It was *nice*. And the complete opposite of how she currently felt. So much of her life was people trying to win her over because of her last name and the reputation that came along with it. But this woman had her arms crossed, and she was openly staring. It was straight up subway etiquette. Her ripped coveralls weren't artful, but well worn, almost like the holes hadn't been there when she bought them. How novel. She had them unzipped to the waist with the arms knotted around her midriff, like she'd stopped midway through undressing. Coveralls should not be sexy. Everything about the woman was starting to feel deeply unfair to Jones. Her t-shirt had a weird pattern, black and purple and green. It reminded Jones of a bowling alley. An establishment she'd been invited to exactly once, and she'd promptly sprained her wrist. After that, Birdie had instituted a strict no sports birthday party and bat mitzvah rule, which was fine by her.

Was the OshKosh B'gosh woman on the crew for one of the shows? That would explain the giant hammer she was dragging behind her. It looked impossibly heavy. Jones wasn't a gym person and had no real concept of weight, beyond the fact that her groceries were always too heavy to carry, which was why she got them delivered.

Stu had kept walking, content to let this woman struggle. How irresponsible. Well, that was a potential workplace injury risk Jones wasn't willing to take the liability for. Not on her first day as interim CEO. Plus, if she offered her help, maybe she could do the impossible and make a friend here, instead of just meeting with weird leering men in bespoke suits.

"Can I help you with that?" Jones stepped toward the woman, before she realized she'd made up her mind. Anything to avoid a lawsuit.

"With what?"

"That, um, hammer? I don't want you to get hurt." That's

right. Jones was calm, logical. She had everything under control.

The woman's voice tipped into laughter. "Sure," she said, her eyes flashing and she flicked her wrist.

Shit. Not even an hour in and she was going to need a hospital. She'd never caught anything in her life, and she definitely wasn't going to start with a hammer. Jones ducked and braced for impact. The hammer glanced off her shoulder, and she waited for the pain to come; for her bones to become dust upon impact. Apparently, there would be a lawsuit after all.

And then the hammer bounced. Because Jones, the most gullible woman alive, was so out of her element that she thought the studio would have a mammoth tool lying around instead of some foam prop.

The other woman gave her a sheepish grin. The green in her eyes bloomed. "Oh, shit, sorry. I thought you'd try to catch it. Not…whatever that was." She gestured vaguely up and down Jones' body.

Jones would not blush. She was in charge today. "Why would I try to catch a hammer? It looks like the ones used to drive stakes on a railroad."

The woman shrugged. "I wasn't around when the first railroads were built. But this is television, baby. Nothing here is real."

She'd delivered that last line with an honest-to-God wink. People who could pull off winking had entirely too much power.

Jones felt rage and embarrassment fighting for prominence. And something else just beneath the surface, something that felt a lot like attraction. Since when was a woman throwing something at her a turn-on? *Say something. Anything.* Jones searched her brain for something quippy. "But *I'm* real." *Ugh, not that.*

Green eyes looked her up and down again before the woman took a step back, then another. "Good to know.

Thanks for offering to help. And sorry for hitting on you, you know… with the hammer."

The woman sent Jones a smirk that she felt low in her stomach. Jones was still watching her incredulously as she started walking and crashed full force into the squishy wall of Stu's body. *This could not be her life.*

"Your father never mentioned you were the chivalrous Haelstrom." A crocodile grin split Stu's face. Jones wanted to throw him back into the swamp.

"I'm surprised he mentioned me at all. But sure, I like to lend a hand when I can."

Something rustled behind them and Jones turned to look. She couldn't help it. The woman was pulling her hair back up into a messy bun, which, in turn, was causing her shirt to ride up and show—

"Yes, I can see that. Or a shoulder, in this case. Do you need some ice for that embarrassment?"

Jones fought back the sunburn feeling rising on her cheeks. She only wanted ice if it was a glacier drifting slowly out to sea with her on it. "Are you ready?"

"If you're sure you don't need medical attention, then I'm glad you're still interested in doing business today, since that's why you're here. Right this way." Stu was looking at her like he knew her, which he didn't. He didn't know a single thing.

"Who was that?" She demanded, forcing some authority into her voice. She needed to get this day back on track, now.

"Oh, no one really. Just Elsie, she works on Fangley Heights, that kids show."

"Doesn't that show have the fourth highest ratings on the network?"

"You should know better than to believe everything you read on the internet, Jones. If you wanted the data, you should have asked me for it. Besides, the show could be even more successful without Elsie Webb."

He held the door to the conference room open for her. Never trust a man who holds a door in such a way that you need to brush past him to enter. Stu had perfected that art. Had he learned nothing from his earlier attempt in the studio? Jones grabbed the door handle from him and pulled it so far open its hinges creaked. *There, enough room for everyone.* As she entered the room, she glanced down the polished table to the owlish lawyer sitting at the end. The space was a portrait of everything she'd never wanted. None of this should be her problem. Not the clothes, or the kid, or the embarrassment still flooding her veins from the hallway incident. Her father hadn't trusted her with anything since she'd bombed her internship. Though it wasn't really her fault that she'd refused to take coffee and lunch orders. Her father had accused Jones of being too much Birdie's daughter. Not willing to do what it took to succeed, just looking for a handout. But she wasn't, not really. She just didn't feel much like his daughter either.

Stu pulled out a chair with a dramatic bow, like it was some kind of gallant offering. Jones pulled out the next one over and sat down. This wasn't some restaurant without prices on the menu. He was not going to be in control of this for much longer.

"Sorry to call you in today, Ms. Haelstrom. If these contracts could have waited, believe me, we would have let them." The man extended his hand toward Jones. His grip was bruising. Like he didn't know the difference between a handshake and arm wrestling. "Chuck Westley. I'm your lawyer, well, the network's, professionally speaking."

Chuck and Stu, unreal. "Sure, nice to meet you. Jones is fine."

"So Joanie, like Chuck here was saying, we've gotta hammer out these contracts. No pun intended. The longer the negotiations drag on, the more tempted the talent will be to ask for more. You wouldn't believe how greedy they are. And believe me, we're already giving them plenty. It's children's television for God's sake and these people are confusing it with art."

"Again, it's Jones. Like I mentioned earlier, I did some research last night. It seems like the Children's Entertainment sector is where we make the majority of our money. Especially through merchandising."

"Like *I* said earlier, you can't believe everything you read on the internet." Stu smirked.

Jones sat up straighter. "Okay, so which part of that was incorrect?"

"None of it, I just meant generally speaking. But sure. It's easy to sell puppets and plush toys to five-year-olds. That's hardly an accomplishment." Stu's eyes shone black. A shark in the water. "I was telling you earlier that the show could be more successful. Your father and I were in early talks about a spinoff without Fangley's character. It would focus on Smirch, Trey's character, he's very popular."

Jones hummed noncommittally as she pulled a notebook from her bag and quickly sketched the path they'd taken through the halls. Stu might have escorted her in, but she'd be seeing herself out.

"I think we have a real opportunity here, Trey could be a star, but instead he's stuck listening to Elsie. We're wasting a lot of potential on Fangley Heights."

"Huh. Noted." Jones gave him a close-lipped smile and pulled forward the stack of contracts Chuck had slid toward her. No part of her wanted to review legalese. But who did? Contracts and terms and conditions, you only read them if you had to. And even then, she only skimmed before clicking accept. "So what exactly do you need from me?"

"Just a cursory review so you can sign off on the terms listed. This is really just following protocol. We've been hammering out these details for weeks. Think of yourself as a rubber stamp. Just a name on the line." The lawyer smiled warmly.

"O-kay," she said slowly, fanning through the top pages of the stack like they were a flip book about to reveal their stop-motion secret to her. "I'm not sure why I'd want to think of myself like that. Anything I should know about this contract for Elsie Webb with the red flag on it?"

"Well, Elsie's a bit of a handful. She got us in some hot water at a charity event last year where she refused to confirm Fangley's orientation," Chuck said.

"She got questions about the orientation of a vampire puppet? A child vampire puppet?" Jones was failing to see how Elsie was to blame in this example.

"I don't think it's unreasonable that people want to know what messages their children are getting," Stu said, his voice getting louder with each successive syllable. "But she made a joke of it. Once Elsie makes up her mind about something, there's nothing that can sway her. Everything becomes a moral issue for her. That night she asked the host why so many adults at the gala were sexually interested in puppets. And then later she apologized for kink shaming and recommended Furry conventions to those interested."

Jones held in a laugh, squinting through the glee that story made her feel. She would have paid good money to have been at that event. "And that bothered you all?"

"Of course it did. She lost us a lot of money, but we haven't figured out a way to do Fangley Heights without her. Anyway, we've had some back and forth on her contract negotiations, but I don't think we'll be getting much more pushback." Chuck pushed his glasses up his nose and flashed a look toward Stu.

Well, that sounded ominous. Stu's obvious push for his nephew Trey was a red flag but unsurprising. In this town flattery and nepotism got you everywhere. But something else felt off about this pressure to sign, too, something lurking beneath the surface of these negotiations. She needed an out with a little time to think, and for once she had one in the form of a probably still sticky little brother. "You know what? I left Bentley hanging out down there, and I don't feel great about that. How about I take these with me and review them tonight?"

"Well, like I said, Joanie—"

Jones cleared her throat and Stu paused as she leveled him with a glare.

"Ahem—Ms. Haelstrom, there's not much for you to review. I've signed off on these terms, and Chuck made them airtight. You giving the okay is just a formality." Stu removed a pen from his pocket and pushed it toward Jones. She slid it back with a single finger. It was unpleasantly warm.

Jones glanced at her map, committing it to memory before snapping her notebook closed. "But a required formality, right? As the current CEO?"

"Interim, but yes. That's technically correct." Chuck nodded.

"Well, the world hinges on technicalities, doesn't it?" Jones lifted the contracts and shuffled them into a neat pile with a few taps on the conference table. The sound was louder than she'd expected, and the nervous look that passed between Chuck and Stu sent a little jolt of power through her. Maybe being temporary CEO of her father's company would have some perks after all. "Okay then. Have your assistant reach out tomorrow, and we can arrange a time for someone to pick these up. I'll leave any changes or clarifications in the margins."

Stu smiled wanly. "Just to be clear, Jones, we really don't have time for changes. Your father felt fine about these. We need to have them wrapped up before Monday, or we'll be in a very precarious position, bargaining wise."

"Well, let's hope no changes are needed then, since I'm not my father and I don't see his signature on these." She dug her heels into the carpet and pushed back from the table, sliding the contracts into her oversized leather purse.

Stu stood quickly, knocking over the bottle of water she hadn't given him a chance to open. "I'll show you out."

"That's not necessary. Just two lefts and a right?" Jones turned and raised her eyebrows at Chuck for confirmation. If she had to look at Stu's slimy face again, she'd need to shower in industrial-strength cleaner.

"You learned your way around pretty fast." Chuck smiled at her, but it was more like a grimace.

"I'm surprised my father never mentioned I'm a quick study. Well then, I'm sure we'll be in touch." She pulled the door closed behind her, wishing she still had that giant hammer to swing.

ACKNOWLEDGMENTS

G, thanks for all you do so I can write terrible jokes on the internet and also in word documents. It's a dream come true. My cats contributed all typos.

B, I hope you find the seltzer water refreshing.

Bryce and Steph you are my friendship inspiration. I love you both.

Luci, your friendship has been such a gift. I can't wait to explore Death Valley and stop at every weird tourist trap with you. Thank you, once again, for all of your help with this book!

Shauna, thank you x 1,000 for being a kind stranger on the internet. You absolutely know what you're doing. Please accept a large cat as a token of my gratitude.

L.I.L.Y., you support me and everyone else. I think you're a superhero. I'm honored to be your friend-wife.

DJs, you are the best thing that ever happened to my writing life. I cherish all of you and our group.

Anna, thanks for encouraging me to write in the first place. I can't believe you're still putting up with me.

Amanda, thank you for your final pass and your friendship (and everything in between). Knowing you has greatly improved my life. SC4E.

Anita, thanks for reading this story and encouraging me.

To all my twitter pals, you make my days brighter and support me at my most absurd. Your friendship is a gift I don't take for granted.

If I forgot anyone it is only because I am very tired.

Most of all, thanks to everyone reading this! None of this would be possible without your support.

ALSO BY LUCY BEXLEY

No Strings

Must Love Silence

Checking It Twice

Just My Type

Flying First

First Day: A Flying First Short

ABOUT THE AUTHOR

Lucy Bexley writes romcoms where queer women trip over things and fall... in love with each other. Her stories balance laughter and love with real-world struggles such as anxiety and addiction. Lucy lives in Boston with her partner, pets, and several cases of seltzer. She's the author of six sapphic romances including Must Love Silence and The Bright Side. When she's not writing jokes in a Word doc, she's writing them on Twitter.

www.lucybexley.com